Watch Over Me
A Watched in Darkness Prequel Novella
V.E. Huntley

Published in the United States by V.E. Huntley

The Cataloging-in-Publication Data is on file at the Library of Congress

Paperback ISBN 979-8-9933217-6-9

Ebook ISBN 979-8-9933217-4-5

Book Design by V.E. Huntley

Book Cover Design by C. David Photography & Design

First Edition 2026

Dedication

To all my dark romance girlies who fell in love with Ricky in Watch Me Break and Watch Me Burn and desperately wanted to know his story.
This is how Ricky arrives at Sage & Summit and develops his legendary boob fetish.
It is absolutely Luna's fault, but Maren is just as complicit.
The darkness is coming.
The stalker is coming.
The bodies are coming.
But before the wolf.
Before the darkness gathers at the edge of the trees.
There's a raccoon who decides he's home, and two women who don't stand a chance.

Content Warning

Please visit my website for the entire list of TWs.

This story doesn't contain many trigger warnings, but there are some dark themes or situations that tie it to the main Watched in Darkness series that may be triggering for some readers: graphic violence, torture, boob molestation by a raccoon, references of animal neglect and/or cruelty that takes place or has taken place off page, medical treatment of abused/injured animals (**NO** on page animal abuse), off page death of an animal from injury.

If any of these are potential triggers for you, please do not read. I won't be offended.

Despite the content/triggers and dark elements in this series, this is a book full of love, laughter, found family, and boobs. Lots of boobs.

At its core, it's a love story. About boobs.

Before the stalker.

Before the bodies.

There was a raccoon with terrible boundaries.

Chapter One

Luna

"So he hasn't pooped in two days, huh?"

The patient on my examination table doesn't acknowledge my question. He lies there on the stainless steel, his quills pressed flat against his small body, and his eyes half-closed, too miserable to bother with the world. I pull on a fresh pair of gloves, studying the dull look behind his eyes and the complete absence of any will to fight. He didn't even protest when Maren lifted him out of his cage. That alone tells me everything.

"Nope." Maren leans against the counter with her arms crossed, her dark curly hair a messy halo as it spills from her ponytail. "Not one prickly poopy pellet."

"How's his intake?"

"Not great. He's eating, but it's a one-way street."

The overhead lights fill the main examination room with a flat, clinical brightness that makes everything look a little worse than it is.

"Did you do an X-ray?"

"Already up." Maren tips her chin toward the wall-mounted monitor.

I cross to the screen and lean in. There's a dense shadow low in the GI tract, irregular at the edges. Not impacted feces, but something else. A fragment, maybe. Organic material. It's hard to tell the exact composition from the image alone, but the shape of it is wrong. My stomach lurches the way it always does when a case pivots.

Shit. I really don't want to do surgery on a porcupine.

"Could be part of a pinecone," I say, more to myself than to her. "Or a dozen other things he found and decided to eat."

"Could be a porcupine bad decision." In the monitor's glass, Maren's mouth curves into a smirk. "They're not exactly known for their judgment. Kinda like us when we've had too many margaritas."

I turn back to the table. He's a male, probably two years old given his size, brought in after a hiker found him disoriented and dehydrated, stumbling along a trail three miles east of here. We'd treated the obvious first. Gave him fluids, rest, and monitoring. Now here we are, with the lights on his insides and an answer I don't love.

"Well." I adjust the gloves on my fingers. "You know what that means."

"I know what it means for you."

"Maren—"

"Nope." She holds up both hands and backs toward the supply cabinet. "I've paid my dues. The beaver last fall? That was a year's worth of penance, minimum."

"You're my vet tech. It's in the job description. The actual written description."

"My job description says I assist the veterinarian. And I'm here to assist." Her brown eyes dance, and a slow grin spreads across her lips, like she's been waiting for this exact moment. "While Dr. Luna engages in some anal play with a porcupine."

"Jesus, Maren."

"What? I'm accurately describing the procedure. No judgment."

She pulls supplies from the cabinet while she says it, setting them on a tray in a little row, then gestures to them with a sweep of her hand.

This is the thing about Maren. She's a force of nature wrapped in scrubs, all competence and absolute certainty. She's been this way every single day I've known her, and she'll be this way at the end of the world. It's the reason I love her even as she makes my eye twitch. It's also why she's the best friend I've ever had.

I carry the tray to the stand beside the exam table. The porcupine's breathing is uneven, but even lethargic and miserable, there is still a beauty about him.

Nature's perfect design for the life he lives, yet here he is on my table because he ate something he shouldn't have. I've never been able to decide if that's tragic or just Tuesday.

"I'm keeping the sedation light. He's backed up enough as it is."

Maren leans an elbow on the counter. "So, I've been thinking about a name."

"Already?" I keep my eyes on the tray as I prepare the enema.

"Yup. It's been forty-eight hours, Lu. Which means it's twenty-four hours past the twenty-four-hour rule. And since it's my turn to name—"

"Do I even want to know?"

"Porky."

I look up to see her grinning.

"Porky the Porcupine." She says it with her chin up, like she's announcing a new monarch, full of sincerity and not a single trace of irony. "It's perfect. It's a classic. It has gravitas."

"It has zero gravitas."

"Anyway, it's your rule. Any animal here past twenty-four hours gets a name. You said it builds connection. You said it reminds us they're individuals and not just cases. You said names have power. That every creature deserves to be seen as a living being worthy of—"

"I know what I said, Maren."

Her grin is triumphant. "Then Porky it is."

I stare at her for a moment. Fifteen years of friendship. Five years of her working beside me in this building, I scraped together from my grandfather's inheritance and enough sheer stubbornness to embarrass a mule. She was here on day one, when we had one enclosure and a borrowed X-ray machine, and no real reason to believe any of it would work. And she's here now, winning arguments about porcupine names.

"Fine. Porky."

I turn back to the tray, reaching for the ketamine and xylazine combination, calculating the dosage against his weight. "Do you think he'll stay calm enough for a direct injection, or should we use the pole?"

Maren tilts her head, considering the porcupine with the careful look she gives every animal she's still getting to know.

"He didn't give me trouble getting out of the cage, but look at his eyes. He knows what's coming. Use the pole."

Maren pulls on the protective gloves, intent on assisting regardless of her earlier speech. I knew she would.

The door swings open, and Tate stands in the doorway, all six-foot-two of him, with his shoulders hunched forward, one hand still on the doorknob, like he's already apologizing for how much room he takes up.

His hair looks like he's been running his fingers through it, pushed up at the crown and flat on one side, and his glasses have slid to their usual position, which is not quite straight. He's got a face that would stop traffic if he had any idea how handsome he was.

Twenty years old, two months into his wildlife biology internship from CSU, and he's one of the best interns we've had since we opened. Right now his bottom lip is tucked in, which means he has news he's not sure how to deliver.

"Luna, Roger just called."

My hands go still over the syringe. Roger works at County Animal Services, and his calls mean a new animal is coming in. And it's always fifty-fifty on how bad it is.

"What's he got?"

"Mom and baby raccoon, found on the side of the road. Hit and run."

My stomach drops straight through the floor.

"How baby are we talking about?"

"He said to get the incubator fired up."

Shit. Depending on the mom's condition, the kit will need supplemental heat around the clock and feeding by syringe every two to three hours.

"How far out is he?"

"Thirty minutes."

I look at Maren. "Go. Get us ready. I've got him."

Her gloves are off, and she's halfway to the door before I'm done talking.

Tate is still in the doorway, his eyes moving around the room, looking like he wants to be useful and isn't sure what to do.

"You want to assist in here?"

He straightens, and his face lights up. "Yeah. What've we got?"

"Luna needs you to shove your finger up—"

"Maren." I point at her, then catch myself and lower my hand. "Go get the incubator prepped."

Her laughter floats back to us as she disappears down the hall. That's the other thing about Maren. She can spend an entire morning needling me and working inappropriate sexual references into clinical conversations, but the second the situation turns serious, she's one step ahead of even me sometimes.

"What do we need to do?" Tate asks.

I gesture him toward the table. "You're about to learn how to give a porcupine an enema."

He rolls up his sleeves. "Cool. Let's do it."

I look down at Porky—God help me, his name has already stuck—and let out a slow breath.

"Alright, buddy. It's just you and me and Tate."

———— ⋘○⋙ ————

The procedure starts fine. Porky goes soft against the table, the ketamine doing its job. I reach for the saline, and Tate puts it in my hand before I finish the motion. He uncaps the lubricant before I ask, moving to the far side of the table, leaving me room to work. I narrate what my hands are doing as they do it, a running thread he can follow without stopping to ask.

"Keep the pressure even and low. Let it do the work for you."

"Right." He watches my hands. "Even and low."

"And whatever you do, don't let go of the—"

He lets go of the speculum.

It slips from his grip and clatters against the table. His hand shoots out at the same time mine does, and for three full seconds we're both gripping it, frozen over the sedated body of a porcupine, staring at each other.

I press my lips together. Not a smile. Definitely not a smile.

"I've got it."

"Sorry. My grip—"

"It happens." I take it from his fingers and set it aside. "Grab a sterile one from the cabinet."

He retrieves it. I tear open the packaging and pass it over.

"Both hands next time. And scoot closer to the table. You're reaching."

He adjusts, replants his feet, and gets back to work without making it a whole thing. That's what separates the interns worth keeping from the ones who aren't. It isn't whether they fumble, but what they do in the ten seconds after.

The procedure continues, Porky's vitals holding steady on the monitor, the beep soft and even.

And then Tate sneezes.

The force of it sends his glasses sliding down his nose. His elbow clips the corner of the tray, and the basin tips, saline slipping toward the edge in a slow, inevitable slide. I catch it with my forearm.

"Oh my god." The color drains from his face and comes back twice as fast. "I'm so sorry—"

"Hey." I right the basin and glance up at him. "Breathe. You're fine. He's fine. The saline's fine." I nod toward the table. "Brace your elbows when you need a hand free. It's a built-in anchor."

He exhales and pushes his glasses up before reaching back to guide the tube.

"I sneezed onto a red-tailed hawk once. Year two." I let the silence sit for a beat. "It wasn't during an enema, but she was not pleased. Neither was my boss."

He snorts, and the redness in his face softens to a warm pink. Good. A tense intern is a clumsy intern, and we've had enough clumsiness for one afternoon.

In the back of my mind, behind the steady motion of my hands as I work, there's a clear picture of Maren's face when she hears about the speculum and the sneeze. She'll have the time of her life with that. She'll bring it up at the worst possible moment, making it bigger, louder, and twice as mortifying as it was. Tate will go crimson all over again, and Maren will love every second.

Poor kid.

I walk him through the rest of the procedure without incident.

By the time we're stripping our gloves off and cleaning the tray, Porky stirs against the table, his quills lifting in a slow, drowsy, reflexive attempt at dignity. I rest two fingers on the back of his neck, and he goes still.

"There you go, bud." I drop my glove in the trash. "You're going to feel like a whole new porcupine soon."

"That was so cool," Tate says. "Like, I know it was only an enema. But you... you knew what to do the whole time."

"It's not my first one." I head for the sink. "And it won't be my last."

"Does it ever stop being awesome like that? Knowing you made a difference in his life. Probably saved it?"

I work the soap through my fingers and look at Porky. His quills lie in neat, overlapping rows, his front paws curling loose at the wrists, and his breathing moving through him in long, unhurried draws. He's going to be fine because of all the places he could have ended up, he ended up here, on this table, this morning.

"It hasn't yet." I dry my hands and turn back. "Why don't you carry Porky to recovery?"

"Porky?"

I give him a look.

"Right." He grabs the protective gloves. "Maren's turn to name."

He cups his hands under Porky's belly, palms up, weight distributed the way I show him. He adjusts, finding the right angle. My eyes stay on his hands, and he glances up.

"Is this okay?"

"You tell me."

He looks back down at Porky, reading the porcupine the way I'd want him to.

"Yeah," he says. "I think so."

That's the part you can't teach. You can walk someone through the quills and the grip. But not the part where he checks Porky's face before he checks mine. That part is either instinctive or it isn't.

"Maren!" I raise my voice toward the wall. The building's walls aren't thick. It's one of its many charms. "Incubator ready?"

She appears in the doorway. The easy teasing is gone from her face, swapped out for the version of her that surfaces when something real is coming.

"Yeah. Roger's eight minutes out."

I follow Tate and Porky down the hall to the recovery den, a long room lined with enclosures that range from the small wire cages we built for finches up to the reinforced cell at the far end, built eighteen months ago following an experience with a grizzly I have no desire to relive.

I hold the cage door open while Tate sets him inside.

"Keep an eye on his vitals for the next hour. Anything shifts, come find me. And be prepared for some poop."

He doesn't laugh as I hope. Instead, he straightens, his expression too serious for his young, handsome face.

"Got it." He looks at me. "You sure you don't need me for the raccoons?"

I pat his arm. "We've got it covered." I head for the door and look back over my shoulder. "You did good in there, by the way. Even with the sneeze."

He grins, and I leave him to it.

Back in the main treatment area, I glance at the clock.

Five minutes.

I check the incubator temperature and nudge it half a degree, lay out the triage supplies in the order I'll reach for them, then stand at the window for four seconds before I go back and check the incubator again. The numbers are the same. I knew they'd be the same. I check them anyway because my hands need to be doing something useful while my brain runs through every possible version of what's coming up the drive.

Neonatal raccoons are built to survive. Everything about their first weeks is designed around a mother's warmth and the hard, relentless push toward life. But that design assumes the mother is there. It assumes no road, no thirty minutes in a county truck between what happened and the place that might undo some of it.

The odds are not what I'd like them to be.

But I've had worse odds.

Outside, the sanctuary grounds stretch toward the tree line in the late morning light, the mountains rising in the distance like protective giants.

Sage & Summit Wildlife Sanctuary isn't a large operation. It grew out of the house my grandfather raised me in after my parents died when I was ten. The buildings are rustic but well-kept, pieced together from the money he left me when he passed five years ago. But it's mine, and it's home, and every creature that comes through these doors has a chance they wouldn't have otherwise.

The crunch of gravel hits my ears. Roger's white county truck comes up the driveway, and I'm out the door before he cuts the engine.

***

Roger Hendricks is a tall man, filling out his uniform with a broad frame that comes from years of wrangling animals that don't want to be caught. He comes around the back of the truck with a towel-wrapped bundle cradled in both hands.

I meet him halfway across the driveway.

"Luna." His voice is rough. "I got here as fast as I could."

"Where's the mom?" I scan the truck bed but see nothing. "Any other babies?"

The line of Roger's jaw hardens. "No other babies. Mom didn't make it. Too much damage. I made the call at the scene."

The air goes out of me. I give it one second, then I reach for the bundle. "Let me see him. Is it a him?"

He nods. "I think so."

The towel is warm from Roger's body heat, and the bundle inside it is so light it takes me a moment to locate it. I pull back the edge, and there he is. Smaller than my palm, eyes still sealed shut, fur so sparse it's no more than a suggestion across his back. His whole body trembles with the effort of each breath.

"Found them on Route 7, just past the Miller farm turnoff." Roger falls into step beside me as I move toward the building. "Someone called it in, but by the time I got there…" He shakes his head. "Whoever hit her didn't slow down."

I don't say anything. The anger is there, sitting below my ribs, but it has nowhere useful to go right now, and I know it. It will come later, in the quiet hours of the night when I replay this moment in my head. Right now, there's only the kit in my hands, the flutter of his heartbeat against my palm, and the work that needs to be done.

"Maren!"

She's there, gloved and ready, the examination table cleared and prepped, and a warming pad laid out. Her eyes go straight to the bundle in my hands.

"Fuck. He's tiny."

"Too tiny. Two weeks. Maybe less." I lay him on the table, peeling back the towel. "We need his temperature up, and we need to know what we're dealing with."

We move the way we always do in moments like this, without discussion or narration, because we've been doing this long enough that the choreography is built into us now. Maren reaches for the thermometer while I start at his head, working my hands along his fragile structure. His skull is intact, with no depressions or swelling. His legs respond when I touch them, a weak flex of muscle that means his spine is okay.

Then I reach his left rear foot.

"Maren."

She looks down.

Two of the toes are crushed. The tissue is already discoloring, the delicate bones compromised.

"Shit."

My mind races through options. Surgery, recovery probability, whether the toes can be saved or whether trying to save them would cost him precious energy he doesn't have.

"The foot can wait. His temperature can't."

"Ninety-four degrees," Maren says, sliding the thermometer free.

Way too low. For a kit this age, this small, hypothermia is as dangerous as whatever injuries he may have.

I reach for my stethoscope. His heartbeat is fast and thready, his body working very hard to stay in the fight.

"Stay with me. Come on, baby."

"I'm gonna go," Roger says from the doorway, and I glance over at him.

"Thank you, Roger. Seriously. Thank you for bringing him to me."

He nods, and I know the look on his face. He did his job, got here fast, drove without stopping, and still ends up standing in a doorway watching someone else do theirs, hoping it's enough.

I turn to Maren. "SubQ fluids. And the smallest feeding syringe we have."

She goes still. "Luna."

"I know."

Her eyes stay on me, reading my face in the way only she knows how. Then she turns and goes for the supplies without another word.

I know what it means. Bottle-feeding means around-the-clock care, every two to three hours, no exceptions. It means sleepless nights and exhausted days, carrying the kit against my body to keep him warm and comforted, becoming his entire world because his mother is gone and there is no one else.

It means falling in love with something that might die anyway.

His paws tremble and curl when I run my thumb across his belly. A reflex. Grasping for the body that should be there.

I've done this before. I've done this and lost them. I've done this and loved them. And I've never once figured out how to stop doing either.

The next hour is a blur of careful work. With the help of the fluids, his color begins its slow return. I clean the damaged foot with a gentleness I have to concentrate on to maintain. Not because I'm careless but because the anger at whoever didn't slow down keeps trying to find its way into my hands. I bandage the toes and set the surgery question aside for later. I check his temperature every fifteen minutes and watch it climb by fractions.

"Ninety-seven," Maren says, at some point that might be thirty minutes in or might be sixty.

I mix the formula with Pedialyte, grateful we have raccoon formula on hand, and warm it to body temperature before loading it into a syringe with a nipple attachment. His temperature hits 97.4, and I let myself exhale. Still not high enough, but we're getting there.

I lift him from the warming pad and tuck him against my chest. His nose twitches. And then, for the first time, he makes a sound, a thin mewling that lasts half a second and undoes the careful control I'm clinging to.

I press the nipple to his lips. "I know you're hungry. Come on. Just a little."

Nothing happens for a long moment. I count the seconds. One. Three. Five. Then his mouth opens.

I press the syringe, and a drop of formula hits his tongue. He swallows, wrong and clumsy, but he swallows.

"There you go." My voice comes out low. "Good boy."

It takes almost twenty minutes to get ten cc into him, but I consider that a victory.

Maren is in the doorway when I look up, arms crossed, her face closed down, set in a neutral expression that takes effort. The easy thing for Maren is to let it all out. That face means she's holding something back.

"You're gonna wear him against your chest, aren't you?"

"He needs a heartbeat. The incubator keeps his temperature, but it doesn't give him a heartbeat."

"Luna." She pushes off the door frame and crosses the room, stopping at the edge of the table. "You did two-hour feedings with that baby squirrel last year. I almost had to hospitalize you because you became an incoherent mess who was convinced Shadow was talking back to you."

"So?"

"In Spanish."

"And your point is?"

She's done the math, and she needs to know I have too. A kit this small, with no mother and no warm body to press against except mine. Her gaze goes to him before she looks back at me and then lets out a breath that could level a building.

"Let me call Estella and tell her I can't make dinner tonight."

My eyes burn and my breath hitches. I can't speak over the lump in my throat. I catch her before she turns, my free arm hooking around her neck, pulling her in. The kit is between us, and I hold my breath as Maren's hands come up around my back, careful not to squeeze too tight, and she holds on.

"Okay, I'm here for this hug, but if this raccoon ends up traumatized by boob contact before he even opens his eyes, that's a new low. Even for us."

A soft laugh slips out, and the pressure behind my eyelids retreats. Maren pulls back and turns toward the supply cabinet.

"I'll head to bed right after dinner. Then I'll take the midnight-to-four-AM feedings. You can have him back at six, when you start your daily impression of a person who's fine."

The knot in my chest loosens just enough to breathe. I don't call it relief out loud. Maren doesn't need me to.

"Thank you."

"Save it." She pulls the overnight supplies together, including the sheets and blanket for the sofa in my office. "We both know you're gonna try to do all the feedings yourself."

She's not wrong. But she'll show up at midnight anyway, eyes half-open, hand out for the kit without a word. She'll do it because that's the part of her that doesn't announce itself. The part that appears when it's needed and doesn't ask to be thanked for it. The one that stays up through the dark hours for an animal she met two hours ago.

Her love for these animals runs every bit as deep as mine. She'd just rather you didn't make a thing of it.

Evening comes in stages this time of year. Gold first, stretched long across the enclosures and the fence lines. Then orange burns the edges of everything it touches. The cool blue-gray comes last, rolling down off the mountains.

I move through my tasks with the kit tucked in the fleece wrap I've fashioned into a carrier, lined with the warming pad. I check on Porky, who's feeling better based on the explosion he had in his cage this afternoon and his increased interest in being uncooperative. Whatever was plugged up there is out now.

I update the charts and respond to three emails I should have answered yesterday. The kit's weight against my chest is so slight I keep checking to make sure he's still there. He is. Rising and falling with my breath, like we've found a shared rhythm.

Maren went to bed two hours ago after making us grilled cheese sandwiches and tomato soup for dinner. Her room has been hers since Grandpa died. She keeps clothes in the dresser, a toothbrush in the bathroom, an absurd amount of hair product in the shower, and a stack of smutty, dark romance novels on the nightstand that she thinks I don't notice. She sleeps here more nights than she doesn't. It's her room, the same way this is her home, even if neither of us says it out loud.

I feed the kit at eight. He eats better this time. He's still weak and clumsy, but his swallowing reflex is stronger.

Shadow lies on the floor beside the sofa as I lean against the arm, legs stretched out in front of me. The kit rests in the valley between my breasts. I'm surprised he was the only kit with the mom. Raccoons have litters ranging from three to five babies. Could there have been others Roger didn't find? Could they still be alive?

At ten he takes even more, and his temperature reads ninety-nine degrees. The breath I've been holding all night comes out in a rush.

His foot is still a concern, swollen and discolored, the tissue around the damaged toes looking worse than it did this morning. I'll reassess it tomorrow and make the call on surgery then. Tonight I'm not asking for much. His chest still moving when morning arrives. That's it.

At midnight, I stand at the window in my office. The kit is asleep, his heartbeat a steady small percussion against my chest. Shadow is asleep on his bed in the corner, refusing to stay in the house. He always knows when I need him.

He came to me the same way the baby now resting against me did, motherless and at the mercy of strangers. I was interning with Fish and Wildlife during my first year of residency, and a call came in about a dead wolf on a trail with a pup nearby. He was trembling, gray and thin, ribs visible under his coat, and ears pinned back. His eyes moved from Roger to me and stopped. I reached into the brush, and he pressed his whole body against my hand.

That was the end of any other life I might have lived.

Grandpa said we should keep him, which was easy to want and harder to arrange. Colorado law treats pure wolves as wild animals, unownable and unclassifiable as pets. A licensed wildlife sanctuary was the only legal route.

He listened with his arms crossed and nodded once. The next morning he was at the county office when the door opened, and by the following afternoon, our land had a new designation. He never mentioned it again.

Outside, the barn and enclosures are quiet, their occupants settled, the paths between them empty in the moonlight. The mountains beyond are a dark mass against a sky dense with stars and an almost full moon.

Past the treeline, where the property butts up against the BLM land, is the Morrison estate. I can't see it from here, but it's almost as if you can feel the heavy darkness of it through the trees. I used to hike in the woods as a girl and sneak onto the property. I couldn't see inside the enormous house. All the windows were boarded up, but something about the property intrigued me. Even with its dark history.

The kit stirs and makes a small sound.

I look down at him, at the sealed eyes straining toward the light they can't yet reach, the injured foot wrapped in a careful bandage, and the paws that curl and uncurl, reaching for a mother who's gone.

"I don't know if you can hear me." The office is still, with only my voice, his breathing, and Shadow's soft snores. "But I'm going to do everything I can for you. You're not alone anymore."

His paw opens and closes against my chest. So small I barely feel it.

"I promise."

"Time's up."

I turn around to see Maren's sleepy face in the doorway. She's wearing flannel pajamas, the ones with the little bears on them that she'd die before admitting she loves. Her hair is a bird's nest around her head, coiled and matted against one side, the other half exploding outward in wild, rebellious brown curls. She's holding coffee in one hand and a formula syringe in the other.

"My boobs are ready. Hand him over, Doc."

Chapter Two

Luna

Maren is on the sofa when I enter my office at six the next morning. She's got the kit draped against her chest, the warming pad resting over him, his face pressed against her skin above her collar, and the syringe between his lips.

She glances up. "You look like hell."

"Good morning to you too."

"Did you even sleep?"

I ignore her question. "How is he?"

"Hungry. He's like most males. All he wants to do is eat. And nice deflection, by the way." Her eyes narrow. "Luna?"

"Hmmm…" I avoid her gaze.

"Don't you hmmm me." She glances at the mud on my boots long enough to make her point, then looks back up at me. "How was whatever insane thing you clearly did last night?"

I pull the boots off at the door and leave them there, then drop onto the other end of the sofa. Shadow pads in from the kitchen, muzzle damp from his water bowl, and settles at my feet with a grunt. I lean down and scratch behind his ears.

"I texted Roger."

Maren arches an eyebrow. "I didn't know you and Roger were texting besties. Should I be jealous?"

I meet her eyes. "I wanted the exact location where he found the kit and his mom."

"Don't tell me you—"

"I needed to know if there were other babies."

"Are you out of your freaking mind?"

She makes a sound in her throat and looks down at the kit. His tiny fist flexes against her in a slow open-close motion, the way young animals do when they find a heartbeat and match its rhythm.

"This animal has been trying to feel me up all night."

"He's kneading. It's a reflex."

"Sure. That's what they all say." She adjusts the nipple when it slips out of his mouth. "He ate great, by the way. And did one very impressive poopy. I almost took a photo, but I showed professional restraint." She shifts him, resettling his weight. "I can't believe you went out there alone. In the dark."

"Shadow was with me."

"Having a wolf doesn't make it safe."

"He's a very large wolf."

"Luna."

My name. Two syllables that are her way of having an argument with just one word. But there's no fire to it. She's not surprised or angry, not really, because she knows me better than anyone else on the planet. She's met every version of me and made her peace with all of them, even the ones that come home at dawn with mud on their boots after digging through brush looking for baby, motherless raccoons.

"Did you find anything?"

"No."

I have mixed feelings about it. I'm relieved I didn't find any dead babies, but I still worry that maybe Mom hid them out there somewhere before she was hit, and I didn't search long enough or far enough off the road. And with the temperatures last night, they wouldn't have survived the cold.

Maren exhales through her nose. "Okay."

I brace for the lecture, but it doesn't come. I look at her sideways.

"Okay?"

"What do you want me to say?"

"Aren't you gonna yell at me?"

"Would it do any fucking good?"

Her voice is cool and detached, but worry still lingers behind her eyes.

Shadow lifts his head, looks at the door for no visible reason, then puts it back down across my feet. The office is hot. We turned the heat up higher than usual, and the warmth has settled into everything.

I hold my hands out to her.

"Can I take him?"

"Yes." She sits forward. "My boobs need a break."

I take the syringe first, then Maren eases the kit away from her skin, one hand under the warming pad, the other supporting him until I'm close enough to take over. He squeaks at the transfer. I settle back into the corner of the sofa, pull him to my chest, and find the spot that worked last night. His nose finds the skin above my neckline, and the squeaking stops. I slip the nipple back between his lips.

Maren stands, stretching her arms above her head with a groan, then disappears into the kitchen. The coffee maker kicks on, mugs hit the counter, and cabinets open and close with slightly more noise than necessary. The kit breathes against my throat, his whole body rising and falling with the simple effort of being alive.

When she comes back, she sets a cup for me on the coffee table and drops into the opposite corner of the sofa, both hands wrapped around her mug like it's keeping her upright.

"He needs a name," she says.

I look down, and his tiny fingers grasp for mine, holding the syringe.

"I'm still deciding."

"I've known him less than a day, and I can already tell he needs a name that'll live up to what's gonna be a big personality." She pulls her feet up under her and regards me over the rim of her cup. "I named Porky. That was a masterpiece, and I stand by it, so you need to bring your A-game. I've got a list."

"Of course you do. Have you been thinking about it all night?"

"Hell ya, I have." She takes a sip of her coffee. "Bandit?"

"No."

"Expected. Don Juan?"

"Vetoed."

She sighs with disappointment. "He's been face-first in my cleavage all night. It fits."

"He's a newborn, Maren."

"Never too early to establish a brand."

Shadow gets up, pads over to her, and shoves his nose into her knee. She rests her hand on his head.

"Okay. What about Fabio?"

I look at her like she's grown two heads.

"Why would I name him Fabio?"

"He's barely got peach fuzz at this point, but he's going to have long, flowing fur. I can feel it."

"No."

She taps her mug. "Okay. Different direction. Thunder."

"He weighs six ounces."

"Thunder isn't about weight. It's about energy."

"He has zero energy. He's barely conscious."

I run my finger over the top of the kit's head, and his ears wiggle.

"Okay, let's go in the opposite direction. Something with class. How about Reginald?"

"I'm not calling a baby raccoon Reginald."

"Lord Reginald of the Trash Heap."

I stare at her, and the corner of my eye twitches. I wait for the punchline, for the tell, for any sign at all that she's pulling my leg.

"Are you kidding me?"

"It's distinguished," she insists.

"It's deranged."

She scratches Shadow's ears. He makes a low sound in his chest and tips his head into her hand.

"Fine. Maximilian."

My head falls back onto the cushion. "No."

"Thaddeus."

"I'm not calling him Thaddeus."

"Why? It's a power name."

"It's a name you give a Victorian ghost."

"Professor Trash Paws."

I lift my head and look at her. "Maren."

"That one was good, and you know it." She points her mug at me. "What's your suggestion then, since you're so picky?"

I look down at him again, at the sealed eyes and the twitching nose, the faint stripe pattern already there in the soft fuzz, like something being slowly uncovered, and the way his whole face is pressed against me like I'm the only warm thing in the world.

"Ricky."

Maren is quiet as she turns her mug between her palms. Shadow's tail sweeps once across the floor and stops.

"Ricky... the Raccoon," she says.

"Don't make it weird."

"Any particular reason, or did you pull that out of your ass when you and Shadow were digging around in the underbrush at two in the morning?"

I take a breath as the familiar ache that never fully leaves me moves through my chest.

"Grandpa found a dog on the side of a highway when I was eight. He named him Ricky."

Maren's eyes soften. They always do when Grandpa comes up.

He found the dog half-starved and terrified and had carried him home in his jacket. Ricky had a black and gray coat that looked almost striped in the sunlight. He lived to be sixteen and slept at the foot of Grandpa's bed every night until the end.

"He just looks like a Ricky."

Maren glances at my chest. "I remember you showing me a picture of that dog. He died right before you came to college, right?"

I nod over the lump in my throat.

"Seems right, I guess." Then the corner of her mouth curves, and I know what's coming. "Ricky. The. Raccoon."

"Don't."

"I'm not doing anything."

"You're spacing them out."

She presses her lips together.

"Okay," she says. "Ricky, the raccoon, it is. Your grandfather would be happy."

"He would."

She lifts her mug toward Ricky in a small toast, and I let myself have the moment before she ruins it.

"It's so bad it's almost good." She presses her fingers to her mouth. "Ricky the Raccoon. Maybe you can give him his own Saturday morning show."

"Maren."

"What?" Her lips twitch again as she chuckles. "Ricky. The. Raccoon."

"You're gonna keep saying it like that until it stops being funny to you."

"I'm gonna say it like that forever because it will never stop being funny to me."

She unfolds herself from the sofa and picks up both mugs, padding toward the kitchen. At the doorway she stops and looks back at us.

"For what it's worth, he looks like a Ricky."

She disappears into the kitchen. Shadow lifts his head and watches the empty doorway until she returns a few minutes later with two fresh cups.

"You let your coffee get cold."

Maren tucks herself back into her end of the sofa as Ricky finishes his syringe. I pick up the next one from the coffee table, milk still bubbling in the fur around his mouth. He latches on before I've fully positioned it, pulling hard, his face scrunched with the effort of eating. His breathing feels better against my skin this morning than it had at midnight, deeper and more even.

I stroke his back with my fingertip as we both watch him eat. His determination is impressive. He wants to live. Maren's eyes drift closed, the night catching up with her.

Ricky uncurls his paw against my chest. All five fingers of one hand spread wide, then press into the soft tissue of my breast, flexing, releasing, and then flexing again.

"Maren."

"Hmmm?" Her eyes stay closed.

"Look."

She opens them, blinking, and looks over at us. I tip my chin down at his hand gripping my breast over my shirt. She watches for a moment, coming back to herself. Then she points at him with one finger.

"Ricky the Raccoon is feeling you up."

"I told you it's a kneading reflex, but he's strong enough to do it now. He wasn't last night."

Maren sits up. "He did that to me for six hours." She gestures at her own chest. "I thought we had a connection."

I pull the syringe away a few minutes later when it's empty. Maren is snoring on the other end of the sofa, and Ricky nuzzles his nose against the swell of my breast, his tiny hand opening and closing. It's faint, the pressure barely there, but it's unmistakable.

Chapter Three

Luna

Ricky has been against my chest since yesterday morning, nestled in the fleece wrap while I moved through rounds and made phone calls and did everything a person does with one hand while the other stays pressed against one hundred ninety grams of raccoon. He fusses when I put him in the incubator, so I've stopped trying.

At my desk, I make it halfway through my paperwork backlog before he starts to move, shifting, his small feet pushing against the flannel wrap in a way that's new. This isn't his kneading reflex or the usual pawing. This is restlessness, his whole body tight with discomfort.

I push back from the desk and carry him down the hall to the main treatment room, passing where Maren is standing at one of the exam tables with Priya beside her, both of them bent over Honey's outstretched foot. She's been showing our intern how to trim our resident rabbits' nails. Flower sits nearby, her nose twitching as she watches her sister. The two rabbits came to us ten months ago, pulled from a breeder in Glen Falls whose idea of animal care was intermittent feeding. The plan had been to rehome them, but Maren and I lasted two weeks before we stopped listing them as available for adoption.

I pull Ricky from the wrap and lay him on a towel over the warming pad. As soon as he's spread out, I notice his belly.

It's rounder than it was at his last feeding, the skin tight and distended. I press two fingers against it, and he wriggles away from the pressure with a squeak.

Not good.

I pull on some gloves and reach for a cotton ball, wetting it with warm water, before starting the stimulation routine, the same gentle circular motion on his genitals that I do after every feeding to encourage his digestive system to do what it's supposed to do.

It takes less than a minute.

The diarrhea is loose and watery. I set the cotton ball down and reach for a fresh one. His gut is only two weeks old, and the milk replacement is the best option available to us, but it's not his mother's milk.

I work through three more cotton balls before I stop. I hold the last one up to the light. Small. Pale. Thread-thin. More than one.

Oh, shit.

I set him down on a clean section of towel, pull off my gloves, and slip on a new pair. I cover him with another towel to keep him warm, then I stand there for a moment with my hands braced on the edge of the table, staring at him. He's been eating like a champ for the past twenty-four hours, but his weight still hasn't increased even one gram. I'd logged it and told myself it was just a matter of time.

But it's not.

Of course he has worms. I'd been holding the dewormer back, waiting for his eyes to open, wanting him stable, hydrated, and stronger before adding another variable to his fragile system. Meanwhile, the worms had other ideas. I strip my gloves again, wash my hands to the elbow, and pull on a fresh pair.

"Maren." She looks over at me. "Worms."

That's all I need to say. She sets Honey's foot down and places the trimmer on the tray before turning to Priya.

"Okay. Put them back in their enclosure. We'll have to finish her later."

Priya nods and gathers the rabbits in her arms. Maren strips off her gloves, drops them, and crosses the treatment room. She grabs fresh ones and two masks, handing one to me.

She looks at the cotton ball I've set aside, then at Ricky.

"Fuck."

"Yeah."

He's huddled under the edge of the towel, his sides rising and falling too fast with the effort of breathing, and one paw curls against the pain in his tummy.

"Poor little guy." Maren straightens and goes into practical mode, which is where she lives best. "Enhanced handling protocols activated. We need to clean everything. And his bedding has to go."

"All of it," I agree.

"We should get Priya in here so she can learn. She needs to understand this isn't like cleaning up after Porky."

Raccoon roundworms are transmissible to humans. Contaminated feces, improper hand hygiene, and surfaces you don't think to wipe down are all dangerous. Children are especially vulnerable, but it doesn't take a child. All it takes is a moment of carelessness, touching your face before you've washed your hands, or missing a surface you should have hit.

Maren calls Priya, and she appears in the doorway a minute later. She points at the box on the wall.

"Mask and gloves first."

Priya does as instructed and comes to stand beside us. She looks at Ricky, at the cotton ball, and then at our faces.

"Roundworm," I tell her. "It changes our handling protocol."

"How?"

"Everything he's touched gets wiped with boiling water and a bleach solution. Surfaces, the incubator, the table, the tools we've used today. His bedding is going in the trash, not the laundry, because the eggs can survive a standard wash cycle."

"Roundworm eggs can stay viable in soil for years." Maren pulls the bleach spray from under the cabinet. "And they're extremely enthusiastic about finding new hosts. So masks and gloves always until further notice. And when you take them off, you wash your hands like you're about to perform surgery."

Priya nods. "What about treatment for him?"

"Fenbendazole. But the dosing for a kit this size is complicated. He's barely half a pound. The margin between therapeutic and toxic doses is razor thin, and his system is already stressed from the diarrhea." I keep my voice level. "We have to get this right."

"Can he handle it?" she asks.

Maren looks at me, her eyes guarded.

"He has to," I say.

❖

I set Ricky in a tray with a clean warming pad and towel as Maren takes the incubator apart and cleans it surface by surface, the bleach smell hitting the back of my throat, making my eyes water. Priya opens the back door before anyone asks, and the cold that comes in off the mountains helps.

I bag Ricky's fleece bedding, the wrap, and anything else he's touched or that has touched him in the last day. Priya follows Maren around with the disinfectant cloth, wiping everything after she's cleaned it with boiling water.

Ricky shifts under the towel. His back legs push against the terrycloth in slow, weak kicks.

"He needs a diaper," Maren says.

Priya turns around. "Why?"

"So we can monitor his output without contaminating everything around him."

She looks down at Ricky, who has gone still again. "Can you even diaper something that small?"

"Yes," I say. "The problem is finding one that fits."

Maren pulls open the supply cabinet and stares into it, hands on her hips.

"Do we have any micro-preemie diapers?" I ask.

"We used the last two for the baby prairie dogs in January. I forgot to reorder." She closes her eyes and sighs. "Well, fuck."

"I wonder if Ethan has any?"

Ethan Caldwell is a friend of mine from vet school who drives up from Estes Park once a week, volunteering his time to help us. He and his brother run a clinic in town.

Maren pulls out her phone and puts it on speaker. Ricky shifts under his towel, and I reach over and tuck the edge back in, trapping the warmth.

Ethan picks up on the third ring. "Hey, Maren. What's broken?"

"I don't only call when something's broken."

"Then you need something." The smile is audible in his voice.

Maren scoffs but doesn't deny it. "We have a neonatal raccoon, confirmed roundworm, and we're out of micro-preemie diapers. You have any at the clinic?"

There's a brief pause. "Yeah. How many do you need?"

"Six. Ten if you have them."

The sound of drawers opening and closing comes through the phone. "I've got a partial box. I'll set them aside."

"You're my second favorite vet."

"Luna's in the room, isn't she?"

"Hi Ethan," I say with a laugh. "Thanks for this. You're a life saver."

"No problem. I'll see you Saturday."

Maren ends the call and scrolls through her contacts. "I'm calling JT."

JT is Maren's live-in boyfriend of almost two years. He drives long-haul, a route that takes him from coast to coast sometimes.

"Isn't he still on the road?"

"He got back this morning."

"Hey babe," JT answers, his voice thick with sleep.

"Hi, baby. Sorry to wake you."

"Mm. Why do you sound weird?"

"I have a mask on." She leans against the counter. "I need a favor."

"That was fast. I've been home less than four hours."

"You love me."

"Yeah." A yawn comes through the phone. "What do you need?"

"Preemie baby diapers from Ethan's clinic."

He groans, and Maren rolls her eyes.

"Can't you get them at the store?"

"They don't sell micro-preemies anywhere locally."

"Why do you need them?"

"You know that baby raccoon I told you about? He's got worms. Can you help us out? I'll make it worth your while tonight."

"Yeah, I'm up." The sounds of him grunting as he gets up filter through the phone. "Give me forty-five minutes."

"You're my hero."

"You always say that."

"I mean it every time. I'll text you Ethan's address."

He makes a sound that might be a laugh, and the line goes quiet.

Priya stands at the counter, her expression a mixture of fascination and the early stages of reconsidering her career path.

"Is this a normal Thursday?"

Maren picks up the bleach spray. "Medium. On a real Thursday, there's also a deer and someone crying over a release. Usually, Luna."

"I don't always cry when I release an animal."

Maren catches Priya's eye and nods.

I look at Ricky, at the labored effort of his breathing, and at his small body working hard to stay alive. The worms explain everything. The weight plateau, the lethargy, the way he eats and eats and still feels hollow against my chest. His body's been fighting on two fronts, and he's been too small to fight on even one.

"Let me figure out the dosing," I say. "I want to get him treated. Maren, can you feed him again?"

"Doesn't that defeat the purpose?" Priya asks. "Won't he just poop it out?"

"We need to keep him eating and hydrated. Dehydration is as dangerous as the roundworm."

Maren heads for the kitchen as Priya reaches for the trash bag. "I'll take this out."

"Don't forget to wash your hands well when you come back in."

After she heads out, Ricky squeaks and squirms under the towel. I pull on fresh gloves and lift the edge of it. I run my finger the length of his spine, and his squirming slows.

"We're gonna get you through this, okay? You're gonna be fine."

Chapter Four

Damien

The world looks better from sixty-three floors up.

I stand at the floor-to-ceiling windows of my corner office and watch Denver spread beneath me, a circuit board of clean lines and patterns so predictable they stopped interesting me years ago. The glass is custom, triple-paned, and tinted, letting me see without being seen. I specified that detail when the Wolfe Group bought the tower seven years ago. The architects balked at the cost. They no longer work for me.

Far below, the midmorning streets pulse with the small, unremarkable movements of people who have no idea they're being watched. A courier weaves between taxis on Seventeenth Street. A woman in a red coat stops at a crosswalk, and two men in suits on the corner are in what appears to be an argument or the performance of one. I watch them with the same detached attention I give everything from up here.

"You're brooding again."

The voice comes from behind me, low, clipped, and carrying the dry observation that only Cade Crawford can deliver without it sounding like insubordination.

"I'm thinking. There's a difference."

"Not when you do it."

My mouth twitches. Not quite a smile, but the closest thing to one that most people ever see. I turn from the window and regard the man who serves as my chief operating officer. He runs all my companies for me and is my conscience—such as it is—and the only person who knows who I am underneath the facade of Damien Wolfe, billionaire mogul and philanthropist.

He's settled into the chair across from my desk, one leg crossed over the other, a tablet balanced on his knee. At six-four, with a physique that his tailored charcoal suit does very little to soften, he occupies space the way a weapon occupies a holster, contained, purposeful, and threatening even at rest.

His dark hair is cut in a short military style, more gray now than black, and the gray has nothing to do with age and everything to do with the things he's seen or done in the service of his country. A thin scar bisects his left eyebrow. Another fainter one traces the line of his jaw from ear to chin. Under his suit are other scars I've only seen glimpses of because he doesn't speak of them, and I've learned not to ask.

On the low sofa along the east wall, Athena snores.

With clean horizontal lines, pale ash, black steel, and a muted indigo silk panel on the north wall, the office is designed with a minimalist aesthetic. She disrupts the geometry, sixty-five pounds of round silver-blue pitbull muscle arranged across the cushions with the relaxed authority of a dog who has decided the furniture is hers and is prepared to defend that position.

Cade glances at her. "She's on the sofa again."

"So?"

"You paid sixty thousand dollars for that sofa."

"She doesn't know that."

He drops his eyes back to the tablet, and his hands scroll across the screen. He's said his piece, and he's done with it. Whatever Special Forces drills into a man doesn't leave when the uniform comes off. It reappears in boardrooms, in civilian attire.

"Quarterly projections for the Foundation." His eyes stay on the screen. "Charitable contributions up eighteen percent. Nine new rescue operations funded this quarter. The board is thrilled." He continues scrolling. "Marketing wants to do a profile piece. 'The Billionaire Who Fights for the Voiceless.' Their words, not mine."

I settle into my chair and straighten my cuffs. The wolf-head cufflinks catch the light, a gift from Cade three Christmases ago, delivered with the deadpan observation that I might as well lean into the branding.

"No. Wolfe Group numbers?"

"Tech division exceeded targets by twelve percent. Defense contracts on schedule. Security division is ahead of projections, but those are the things that can wait."

I lean back. "And the things that can't?"

Cade sets the tablet down. His flat, gray eyes meet mine, assessing me the same way he does everything. He sorted the world into threats and non-threats a long time ago and hasn't revised his system since.

"Victor Briggs."

I press two fingers into the edge of the desk, the carved walnut biting into the pads of my fingertips.

"What did you find out?"

His jaw tightens, a compression so slight most people would miss it. "Running a video operation out of a warehouse in Commerce City. Animals on camera, packaged and sold on the dark web to people who pay a premium for that specific category of content." He stops, then starts again. "The animals don't get veterinary care after. They get a bolt gun if he's feeling generous."

Heat moves through my chest in a slow black wave. Under my fingers, each ridge and knot where the wood is joined presses into my fingertips.

"How many?"

"Thirty-eight in the current rotation. Mostly dogs. The DA's office has had a file open for fourteen months. Briggs' brother-in-law is a deputy in Commerce City PD. The legal system won't touch him."

The legal system. I almost laugh. Half the states in this country classify animal cruelty as a misdemeanor, handing out fines and probation to men who starve horses to skeletons, run puppy mills in their basements, and pour acid on cats for entertainment. The system is a joke written by people who have never looked into the eyes of a dying animal and seen their own helplessness reflected back.

I have. I was nine years old when I learned what people were capable of doing to animals.

"Tonight."

"I figured." He turns the tablet to me, and a satellite image fills the screen, annotated in red and blue, showing approach vectors, exit routes, and intercept points. "Briggs leaves Commerce City around ten-thirty. Takes a rural stretch of Picadilly Road to a rental in Aurora. No cameras for a two-mile corridor. Nearest neighbor a quarter mile past a treeline. Option two gives the most time and the cleanest extraction route."

I study the screen. Cade's work is always immaculate. It has to be.

"And the animals? After?"

"Anonymous tips to three separate rescue organizations, staggered by three hours. The warehouse gets hit within six hours of Briggs going dark."

"Cleanup?"

"Same protocol as Jennings." He says it with the detached professionalism of a man discussing quarterly revenue projections. Which, in a sense, he is. This is the other side of the ledger, the one that doesn't appear in any Wolfe Group financial statement. The one that exists only between two men who made a pact years ago over a bloody sink.

I straighten my tie, a small, centering gesture.

"Good. What's next?"

We're twenty minutes into defense contract renewals when my phone buzzes against the desk. Elise Whitfield, Pinnacle Realty. In the last three months she's shown me seven properties, none of them right.

The specifications I gave her are honest, which is the problem. What I need doesn't translate into listing criteria.

I hold up a finger, and Cade leans back in his chair.

"Elise."

"Damien, I hope I'm not interrupting."

"What can I do for you?"

"I know it hasn't been an easy search, but I think I might have found the right property."

"I'm listening."

"It's in Aspen Ridge. Thirty minutes north of Estes Park. Five hundred acres, Victorian estate, completely secluded. Bordered by BLM land on three sides. Privacy. Acreage. Distance from neighbors. It checks every box you gave me."

Privacy. Acreage. Distance from neighbors. The polite translation of what I told her.

I want to be left alone, and I want anyone who comes anyway to have to work for it.

"What's the catch?"

Papers shuffle through the line. "It's been on the market for years. Multiple price reductions. The property is extraordinary, but it has a history." She pauses. "A sordid one. Most buyers won't even drive up."

Across the desk, Cade has stopped scrolling.

"Elise," I say, and the line goes quiet. "Sordid doesn't bother me."

She releases a breath that sounds relieved.

"I could meet you there this afternoon. Three o'clock?"

"Send me the details."

I end the call. Her text arrives a moment later, and I slide the phone across the desk to Cade. He reads it, forwards it to his own phone, and hands it back.

"I'll pull everything on the property."

"And the town."

Cade nods, and the tablet comes back up. The conversation is over, and he's somewhere else in his head, which is what I pay him for.

The sofa cushion exhales as Athena drops to the floor. Her nails are quiet on the hardwood, just the faintest tick with each step. She sits at my knee and looks up, her eyes soft and trusting, the way only a dog can look at a person who has never once given her a reason not to.

Two hours northwest of Denver, the twenty-first century starts falling away.

Interstate 25 feeds into a state highway that narrows like a funnel, squeezing the modern world out mile by mile. The strip malls thin, the billboards disappear, and the guardrails go from steel to wood to nothing at all.

Athena has her nose wedged into the two-inch gap that I've left at the top of the passenger window, highlighting the scarring along her muzzle where the skin never grew back right. Two years out of the fighting ring, and she still does this on every long drive, as if she were on her freedom ride.

"You're going to freeze your face off."

She pulls her nose in from the window and sets her head on my thigh, her eyes closing. My hand drops to scratch behind her ears.

We pass through Estes Park, the town spreading wide after the canyon's compression. Gift shops and outfitters and restaurants with names involving some combination of "elk," "peak," and "lodge."

Within four blocks, the retail frontage thins. Within half a mile, Estes Park is behind us, and I can breathe again. It happens every time the density of other people drops below a certain threshold. It's not misanthropy. Or not only that. It's a preference so deep it lives in my bones, one I stopped apologizing for long enough ago that I've lost the memory of my last apology.

Fifteen minutes north of Estes Park, the road narrows again. The shoulders shrink, the lane markers fade, and the trees press closer.

Then Aspen Ridge appears below.

It sits in a mountain valley like a photograph taken in another era and never updated. A main street flanked by clapboard and brick-front buildings from a century that believed in cornices and hand-lettered signs. The town is picturesque in the way small, forgotten places are, beautiful and irrelevant, and populated by people who know each other's business with the intimacy of a shared disease. A community this close would have disqualified a location before I finished reading the listing because small towns watch, small towns talk, and small towns remember.

But small towns with dark histories have blind spots that are deliberate. Wounds they've scarred over with silence and the unspoken agreement that some things are better left alone.

The property sits ten miles north. The driveway appears. There's no sign or marker, only a break in the treeline and a track cutting into the pines, with dirt and packed gravel, rutted from winter freeze and thaw cycles. I turn onto it, and the Range Rover's suspension absorbs the transition from pavement to packed earth. Stones ping against the undercarriage, and branches crowd both sides close enough to scrape the mirrors.

Good. Every pothole and unmarked foot is a deterrent.

Five hundred feet in, a rusted gate hangs open on broken hinges. Beyond it, the track firms up. Then the trees open without warning.

One moment we're driving through a tunnel of pine and bare aspen, the branches interlacing overhead, and the next, the forest pulls back like a curtain, and the Morrison estate fills the windshield.

It sits on a natural plateau, elevated above the surrounding terrain as if the mountain pressed it up for examination. Three stories of dark timber and stone. Victorian in its architecture, with a wraparound porch, spires on each corner, and windows arranged across the facade with the symmetry of a face that has forgotten how to arrange itself into an expression. The gingerbread trim and decorative brackets of its era are still there, but time, altitude, and neglect have stripped the charm from them.

The mountains rise behind it on three sides, and a pair of ravens sits on one of the turrets, their calls carrying across the distance.

I park beside a silver BMW and cut the engine. The wind through the trees, the slow drip of snowmelt off the eaves, and the ravens above trading insults replace the sirens and traffic I left in the city.

I sit for a moment, letting the quiet settle over me the way it always does when I find the right kind of alone. My hand finds the back of Athena's neck. She leans into it, her eyes on the house.

The front door opens, and a woman steps onto the porch.

Chapter Five

Luna

I run my finger down the dosing chart a second time, then a third before I pick up the syringe. I draw the medication up to the line. The ratio has to be exact. Too concentrated and his system won't be able to handle it, but too diluted and it won't do what it needs to do.

I add it to the formula and swirl the bottle in slow circles. Ricky is tucked against my chest in a new fleece wrap, a cocktail napkin folded and taped around his bottom in something that resembles a diaper the way a paper airplane resembles a 747, but it'll work until JT gets here.

We sent Priya home, and Maren canceled the other interns for the next few days, keeping it to the two of us until Ricky's treated and we're sure the round-worm doesn't spread.

He roots against my collar, his face pressed to the warm swell of my breast. I guide the bottle to his mouth, and he latches on.

The formula should be sweet enough to cover whatever bitterness the treat-ment carries. He pulls at the nipple with those small, concentrated tugs, each one a little stronger than the last. His eyes are still sealed, but I can see the strain of them, the way the lids look tight and thin. Another day, maybe two, and they'll open. He wants to see the world, but his body is not quite ready.

I refuse to let myself think too far ahead. That's the deal I make every time, with every animal that comes in at this stage. One bottle at a time.

The front door opens. JT's footsteps are distinct, heavier than Maren's, and unhurried. He pushes through the double doors from the lobby a second later, a plastic grocery bag dangling from one hand, his jacket half-unzipped, and his blond hair still showing the impression of a pillow. His eyes find mine where I stand beside the counter, and he grins.

"Got your diapers." He lifts the bag.

"Thank you." I adjust the angle of the bottle. "Maren's in the kitchen."

He crosses the room and sets the bag down, peering at the bundle against my chest with genuine curiosity.

"How's he doing?"

I open my mouth to answer, but Maren appears in the doorway, drying her hands.

"You're here." She crosses the room and tilts her face up. "Thanks, babe. You're the best."

One of his hands finds her waist as he kisses her. He pulls back and looks over her shoulder at me, his face scrunching in confusion.

"What the hell is he doing?"

I glance down. Ricky's paw is spread across my chest, his tiny fingers pressing and releasing against my breast through the fabric of my shirt.

Maren snorts out a laugh. "He's been doing that to both of us since yesterday. He's a little perv."

JT's mouth pulls up at one corner. "Can't blame him. You've got fabulous tits."

"Hey, now, boob commentary is my thing." She grabs JT's elbow. "Get out of here. I have work to do. I have to stay up here for a few days, so you're gonna have to take a rain check on my making it worth your while."

She steers him back toward the hallway, talking low and close the way they do, their words blurring into something private.

"See ya, Luna," he calls back over his shoulder.

"Thanks again, JT."

He laughs as the front door opens and closes, and the building goes quiet.

Ricky is still eating, still pressing his palm against me with that same slow rhythm, his nose pressed to my skin, his body curled toward the warmth of mine.

"That's a good boy."

When the bottle is empty, I draw it out and set it on the towel beside me and shift him so I can see his face. The closed eyes, the twitching nose, and the faint tremor of his breath.

Those eyes need to open. He needs to get through tonight and the next one and the one after that. The medication needs to work fast enough, and that small body needs to stop fighting itself and start fighting back.

My fingertip traces the line of his spine, and he arches into it in a gesture of pure trust.

"You're going to be alright," I tell him.

I mean it. I want to mean it. But I've said those words over enough small bodies that wouldn't make it to know what they're worth.

His paw opens wide against my chest. Five tiny fingers. He holds the position for a moment, palm flat against me.

Then his fist closes, his small nails dig in, and he holds on.

Chapter Six

Damien

Elise Whitfield is a woman who makes commission look like a lifestyle choice rather than a financial necessity.

Mid-thirties, dark hair pulled back in a twist that is both professional and suggestive, and a navy blazer over a silk blouse that costs more than most realtors make in a week. She's wearing heels on a mountain property, which tells me she either underestimated the terrain or overestimated the importance of her calves. Knowing Elise, it's the latter. And she's not wrong. They're excellent legs.

Her smile as I step out of the Range Rover is her standard professional smile, but there's a tightness at the corners that I haven't seen before.

I lift Athena out of the passenger seat and set her down. She moves to my left side and sits, pressing against my leg, surveying Elise with the calm attention she grants every new person.

Elise extends her hand, leaning forward so I can take it and kiss her cheek at the same time.

"Damien." She glances down at Athena. My girl's tail thumps once. "Is she—"

"She's fine. She goes where I go."

Elise straightens, the tightness at the corners of her smile smoothing out. "I can't believe you were willing to make the drive."

"Two hours is nothing if the property is right."

"Well. Let's find out."

She leads us up the porch steps, her heels clicking against the wood. The planks are weathered, the grain raised and splintered where water has worked its way in over decades. The wraparound porch is wide with turned balusters in a pattern that still shows in the few that remain.

Athena shuffles beside me with her nose low, sniffing the boards as we cross them.

"The estate was built in 1892 by Harold Morrison." Elise's eyes sweep the property. "Mining money. Silver, mostly. The original parcel was over two thousand acres, but it's been subdivided over the years, most of it folded back into BLM land. What remains is five hundred and seven acres, most of it forested, with the nature preserve bordering three sides."

The hinges protest when she pushes the door open. The smell that comes out is old wood and settled dust, years of it, undisturbed. Athena stops at the threshold, nose angled into the open doorway.

"Seven bedrooms, four full baths, two half baths. Original hardwood throughout."

Elise gestures at the foyer as if the house can speak for itself. It can.

The entry is a cathedral of dark wood and faded grandeur. A staircase splits at a landing before continuing to the second floor in two symmetrical flights. The banisters are hand-carved walnut. The wallpaper is original, a deep burgundy damask faded to the color of dried blood where light reaches it and dark as a bruise where it doesn't. A chandelier hangs from the ceiling three stories above, its crystal pendants dulled by decades of neglect, catching enough light from the transom window to throw faint, dirty rainbows across the walls.

Athena sits at my feet, looking up at the chandelier as I stand in the center of the foyer and listen. The house breathes around me, settling timber, wind finding gaps in the window casings, and the creak of a structure that has been holding its own weight for over a hundred thirty years and is beginning to feel the effort.

"It needs work." The brightness in Elise's voice thins out. "Significant work. But the foundation is solid. Structurally, it's sound."

She sets her leather portfolio on the dusty console table beside the door and folds her hands in front of her.

"I want to be transparent with you, Damien. I almost didn't bring this listing to you. My broker told me I was insane for even considering it. But you've been very specific about what you want, and this property checks every single box. And I believe in giving my clients complete information and letting them make their own decisions."

I know what she's about to tell me. Cade gave me the rundown on the drive, but I'm curious how she'll present it.

"Just spit it out, Elise. I'm not a delicate flower."

Her blood-red lips curve because that's an understatement, and we both know it.

"Morrison raised his family here. His great-great-grandson, Jeremiah, grew up in this house. By all accounts, he was troubled. There were incidents when he was young. Animals going missing in the area. Behavioral issues at school. The family had money, so they managed the problems rather than deal with them."

She pauses.

"In 1982, a sixteen-year-old girl named Sarah Dunning went missing from Aspen Ridge. She was the first. Over the next two years, six more teenage girls disappeared from towns across the region. Estes Park. Loveland. Fort Collins. One from as far away as Greeley." Elise's voice is flat, reduced to the careful monotone of someone reciting facts they'd rather not know. "Jeremiah was arrested in 1984. They found remains on the property. All seven girls."

The chandelier sways in a draft I can't feel, its crystals clicking against each other like the sound of small bones.

"He brought them here and killed them in the basement."

Her eyes cut to the floor and then away. I wait because I know she has more to say.

"He was convicted on seven counts of first-degree murder and died by lethal injection, though that was too good for him, given what he did to those girls." A brief shudder moves through her. "His parents died of a double suicide six months after the execution. The estate passed through a series of trusts and holding companies. No one has lived here since 1987. The property has been listed and delisted four times." She meets my eyes. "People in Aspen Ridge call it the Morrison place, and they don't say it the way you'd talk about any other old house. They say it the way you'd say the name of an entity you're trying not to summon."

I let the silence hold for five seconds. Ten.

"Let's see it."

<hr>

Elise leads us through the ground floor, a maze of interconnected rooms. The parlor and a formal dining room with a table that seats sixteen still sit in place under yellowed dust cloths. A study with floor-to-ceiling bookshelves. There's an outdated kitchen, a smaller dining room, and a breakfast nook at the back of the house with windows on three sides.

Athena moves through each room at my heel, her nose sniffing the baseboards and corners.

"Nothing's updated," Elise says. "It would likely need to be gutted."

I nod, running my hand along the doorframe.

"What about the basement?"

Elise's composure fractures for one second. She swallows and shifts from one heel to the other.

"The room he killed them in was dismantled during the investigation. There's nothing left down there but the raw space itself."

"Show me."

The basement door is at the end of the hall beside the kitchen, original, solid oak, with a deadbolt that is not original. The air that rises from below is ten degrees colder than the rest of the house and carries the smell of stone, standing water, and time.

And underneath all of it, the faint smell of copper permeates the air. Blood that has soaked so deep into stone that no amount of cleaning reaches it. The smell of a place where irrevocable things happened, and the walls absorbed it the way they absorb cold and damp. With equal permanence.

I go first. Elise follows, her heels clicking on each step. Athena descends at my left, her nails quiet on the narrow treads, her shoulder against my calf. At the bottom she stops, sitting at the foot of the stairs, and her gaze sweeps the space once and then settles on me.

The basement runs the full footprint of the house. Stone walls, a concrete floor, and load-bearing pillars of mortared stone divide the space. A furnace the size of a small car squats in one corner, and a pegboard lines the adjacent wall, the outlines of tools still visible in the dust like chalk marks around bodies. A hammer here, the spread arc of a handsaw there, and smaller implements in a row whose shapes I note without being able to name a single innocent use for them in this room.

There's a drain under the single long, boarded-up window, a small hole in the right corner where the wood looks eaten away, perhaps by mice. And against one wall is a rickety wooden workbench that's seen better days, the top stained in patterns that no one would call rust.

The center of the room stops me. A long, metal table, such as those in morgues and areas where no one is supposed to know what happens. A single bare bulb hangs above it from a twisted cable. The light hits the surface and returns flat and clean, revealing the brilliance of metal designed for repeated cleaning and the removal of evidence. Morrison put thought into this table and chose it for precisely what it implies.

I glance over my shoulder. Elise hasn't moved from the bottom step, her portfolio held against her chest like a shield. She clears her throat.

"They removed it as evidence during the trial. When it was over, his family requested it be returned." She takes a quick breath. "I have no idea why. It's possibly the creepiest thing about a very creepy property, and that's saying a lot."

I cross to the table and stand at its head. The drain at the opposite end is a small dark circle. The channel around the edge is perhaps an inch wide and an inch deep.

Every measurement in this room is clear to me. The distance from the table to the stairs, the angle of the floor, and the depth below grade. The soundproofing that packed earth provides on all sides and the isolation that ten miles of bad road and five hundred acres of forest provide above that.

I stand in the center of Jeremiah Morrison's killing room and feel nothing.

That's not true.

The blood in the stone. The silence. The table under my hand, the drain at the end of it, and the walls that absorbed everything that happened here and kept it without apology. My pulse is steady. My breathing is even, every nerve in my body is awake and reading this room, and what moves through me has nothing to do with horror or revulsion. It's older than both of those and more fundamental. It's the cellular recognition of a predator standing in a room that was built for exactly the kind of thing he is.

Athena watches me from the foot of the stairs, her eyes level in the half-dark. She's the only creature on earth who sees gentleness from my hands, and she's watching with eyes that hold complete trust.

I turn to Elise.

"Show me the rest."

***

The terrace runs the full width of the back of the house, its stone slabs tilted and separated where the ground has shifted underneath them, but the underlying structure still holds. I stand at its edge and let the property unfold.

The plateau extends perhaps two acres in every direction before the terrain begins to slope, and then the forest takes over, pine and spruce at the lower elevations, their canopy dense enough that the ground beneath them is in permanent shadow, and aspens higher up in stands so thick their white trunks look like bones stacked against the mountainside.

Above that, rock and snow and sky.

Athena is off the terrace, moving through the dead grass and patches of snow at its edge with her nose down. She makes her way toward the tree line without urgency, reading whatever the ground has been holding under the snow.

"What's the deal with the BLM land?"

Elise stands beside me with her portfolio open, one hand anchoring the pages against the wind that has picked up from the northwest. "Bureau of Land Management controls about twelve hundred acres on three sides of the property. Designated wilderness, so no development. No road access. The only way onto the Morrison parcel is the driveway you came in on."

"One route in. One route out."

"Correct. The main road dead-ends at a trailhead a few miles past the driveway. Very little traffic. Hikers in summer, the occasional hunter in fall. Most people head into Rocky Mountain National Park instead."

Athena reaches the treeline. She stops at the edge and turns to look back at me across the yard and then pushes into the pines and disappears.

"Nearest neighbor?"

"The only adjacent private property is to the west. A wildlife sanctuary. Small operation, run by a local vet. You wouldn't have passed it. The GPS routes you on the southern approach, and their access is further north." She waves toward the western treeline. "I wouldn't consider it a concern. The properties don't share a property line. There's a significant buffer of forest between the two parcels."

Animals for neighbors instead of people. They don't talk, don't photograph, and don't stand at a window at three in the morning wondering why the lights in the basement are on.

"How significant?"

"At least half a mile of dense woods. You'd never know they were there." Her lips curve into a smirk. "Honestly, Damien, the sanctuary is the best possible neighbor for someone with your privacy requirements."

Athena comes out of the trees, her muzzle dark with earth, and we circle back to the front. The afternoon light has shifted, the sun dropping toward the western peaks, and the house throwing a long shadow across the drive.

Athena walks to the Range Rover and sits beside the front tire, her tail sweeping the gravel in long, even strokes.

I stand beside her and look at the Morrison estate.

Eight thousand square feet. Five hundred acres. One road in, one road out. BLM wilderness on three sides. A town ten miles south that has spent forty years training itself not to look in this direction. A basement with walls thick enough to contain anything, a history dark enough, and a reputation toxic enough that no one will wonder why the new owner values his privacy.

"What are they asking?"

Elise consults her portfolio, though I have no doubt she has the number memorized. "One point six million. Down from the original ask of three point eight. The trust that manages the estate is very motivated to sell."

One point six million for five hundred acres and a house that would cost thirty million to build today. The discount is the history. Seven dead girls and a name that makes the people of Aspen Ridge look away.

"I'll take it. Full asking price. Cash. Thirty-day close. No contingencies."

Her composure holds, but her eyes widen by a fraction of a millimeter. She was prepared for negotiation and hesitation, not for "yes" before she'd finished making the case.

"Damien, are you sure? We haven't discussed renovation costs, permitting, the history—"

"I'm not most buyers, as you know, Elise." I open the passenger door and lift Athena onto the seat. She turns once and settles into the leather. "Under my name, not Wolfe Group. No public record of my company attached to the property. Cade will send you the details."

"Of course. But your name is well-known. Unless you use an anonymous entity—"

"I don't care if people know I bought it, but I don't want it tied to my business the way my other properties are."

"Understood." She's writing, professional instinct overriding whatever is churning behind that polished facade. "I'll have the paperwork to you in a few hours."

I settle into the driver's seat. Athena presses her nose to the window gap as Elise drives past. Through the windshield, the Morrison estate watches me with its rows of dark windows, every room a rectangle of black in the fading afternoon light, the trim casting thin shadows across the stone facade, the ravens motionless above it all.

Athena pulls back from the window and rests her head on my thigh again.

I pull down the rutted driveway, the branches scraping the mirrors, the potholes jarring the chassis. In the rearview mirror, the house shrinks between the trees. The forest crowds in from both sides, and the gap narrows.

Then the pines close over it, and the Morrison estate is gone.

Chapter Seven

Luna

Five days changes everything and nothing.

Ricky is still small enough to cup in both palms, still fragile enough that I check his breathing before anything else every time I pick him up. But his eyes are open now, two dark beads that track movement and light with an alertness that wasn't there before, and when I hold the bottle out, he goes for it instead of waiting for me to coax him.

His diarrhea has cleared up, and he's stopped passing dead worms in his poop. He'll need to be treated again because the treatment only kills adult worms, leaving the larvae to mature. Additional treatments are always required, but the lethargy that had him limp and unresponsive in my hands five days ago is gone. He wants to move now, wants to explore, and pushes against my palm when I try to keep him still for his daily weigh-in. His temperature is still erratic, but his weight is up two hundred twenty-five grams. Half a pound.

I wrote it in the chart like it was a landmark, because it is.

He's against my chest, as always, bundled in the wrap, the warming pad tucked around him, and he's eating well, one paw braced against my thumb, the other against my breast. The evening light filters through the office window, and it smells like bleach and the coffee I made an hour ago and forgot to drink.

Ricky shivers.

It moves through him in a slow wave, his whole body tightening with it. I pull the wrap tighter, pressing him closer, but it comes again, another tremor rolling through him against my palm.

The smell of pizza arrives before Maren does.

She comes into the office with a flat box balanced on one hand, her purse sliding off her shoulder, and her cheeks pink from the cold outside. She sets the pizza on the desk and looks at us.

"We're eating in here, right?"

I nod. "Yeah."

"How's he doing?"

"He's shivering." I look down at him. "Even in the wrap."

She shrugs off her coat and drapes it over the chair, heading to the door again.

"He was doing it earlier too. Had the warming pad on him and everything."

I pull the wrap back and look at him, at the fine trembling that moves through his small body even as he keeps eating, determined and oblivious to anything other than the nutrition he's sucking down. His dark eyes blink in long, slow intervals, and his nose twitches, but the shivering won't stop no matter how tight I press the fleece around him.

I pull the bottle away, and he chirps in protest, grabbing for it with both hands. I unbutton the top two buttons of my flannel with one hand, keeping him steady with the other. Then I ease him out of the wrap and tuck him inside the collar of my shirt, settling him against my body, the fabric closing back over him.

His tiny fingers grasp my thumb again as he drinks. It takes half a minute, but the shivering slows. Then it stops.

Maren comes back into the office carrying two bottles of iced tea and looks at my chest, watching the small lump of raccoon wriggle under my shirt.

"How long have you two been together?"

"He's cold."

She drops onto the opposite end of the sofa and flips the pizza box open on the cushion between us.

"Whatever helps you sleep at night."

Ricky's free paw wanders across my chest in a slow, uncoordinated pass, not sure how to use his limbs yet. He pats my collarbone before sliding down the slope of my breast, closing around nothing until he finds the top edge of my bra and wraps his fingers around it.

"JT left okay?"

"Yeah." Maren pulls her knees up and grabs a slice of pizza. "He'll be gone ten days. Maybe more if the pickup in Memphis gets pushed."

She handles JT's absences the way she handles most things, by filling the space with noise and motion and staying overnight with me.

Ricky finishes his bottle. I pull it free, and he moves against my skin in the gap, his nose pressing into the dip between my breasts, searching. His fingers press into my breast, flexing, the grip stronger than it was five days ago. Everything about him is stronger than five days ago.

I carry him to the bathroom and run a cotton ball under warm water before rubbing it over him. His back legs kick out, and he pees, a tiny insistent stream, his whole body relaxing around the relief of it. With baby raccoons, you have to stimulate them to go after every feeding, the way their mothers do in the wild, or they'll hold it until they're in pain. I put a clean diaper on him. He'll wear them until I'm sure his roundworm is gone. Then I tuck him back into my shirt and head back to my office.

"I'm sorry you had to stay up here this week while JT was home."

"He's a big boy. He can take care of himself." She takes a bite of pizza and talks around it. "And I got my dick fix Sunday afternoon, so I'm good."

I ease onto the sofa, keeping my free hand on Ricky.

"So…" She finishes the slice and reaches for another. "The usual shifts tonight? 6 hours each?"

"Yeah, I'll take first if you want to sleep."

She pauses chewing. "I don't mind—"

"You drove to town and back for dinner and the mail. I've got it."

She nods. "Okay."

I run my thumb across the top of Ricky's head, and he grabs it with both hands and pulls it to his mouth. His lips close over the tip, and he sucks, eyes drifting shut. Raccoon kits suckle for comfort the way human babies do. He reaches for my fingers constantly now, full belly or not.

"His thermoregulation still isn't where it needs to be. We need to use the warming pads all the time."

Maren nods at my chest. "It seems like he's got his own system figured out, though."

Ricky chooses this moment to release my thumb and push his face above my collar, rooting around with focused intent. His damp nose presses against my skin as his paw flexes against the outer curve of my breast.

"He sure is persistent."

"He's looking for his mom."

"He's looking for something." She gestures at him with the crust of her pizza. "Those eyes are open now. He knows what he's doing."

He does look more purposeful than he did a week ago. His dark eyes stare at nothing in particular, but the rest of him is focused. He turns his face against my chest, settles his chin against the top of my bra, and goes still except for the paw.

The office is warm, the heat turned up the way we've kept it all week, and outside the window the mountains have gone dark blue in the fading light. Maren holds out both hands.

"My turn. You need to eat."

I pull him out of my shirt, lifting the wrap over my head at the same time. He squeaks in protest as the air hits his body. She takes him with both hands, and I help her slip the wrap over her head, tucking him inside as she pulls him to her chest. He roots his face against her, pushing his nose into the dip of her neckline, both paws gripping the shirt over her breast. He makes a low churring sound that he started doing the past few days, a small and continuous sound I have no word for except contented.

He starts to shiver again. Maren looks down at him and then pulls the collar away from her body.

"Yeah, yeah. Get in here."

She tucks Ricky inside, guiding him down against her skin the same way I had him, and his little body goes still the moment his fur meets her flesh. Then the paw comes up, and I can see the shape of his fist flexing through her shirt, the same slow, repeating squeeze he does to me.

The corners of her mouth pull into a smile, the unguarded one she doesn't let many people catch.

"Oh, you're a smooth one, aren't you?"

I take a slice of pizza as Maren adjusts him so his head is poking out of the top of her shirt, but he keeps his grip on her breast and closes his eyes.

Chapter Eight

Luna

Three weeks of no sleep turns a person into something feral.

I know this because I catch my reflection in the dark window of my office at 2:47 A.M. and don't recognize the woman staring back. Hollow eyes, hair escaping its knot in every direction, and a crust of formula dried on my collarbone where Ricky spit up an hour before. I look like a stray animal the sanctuary rescued, not the woman running it.

Against my chest, tucked inside the wrap that Maren and I have been sharing in shifts since he arrived, Ricky churrs in his sleep. His body temperature has regulated itself, so he doesn't need our body heat anymore, not the way he did in those first days when we kept him inside our shirts. But he often finds his way down there anyway, and neither of us has the heart to stop him.

Tonight I've managed to keep him in the wrap, his small clawed hands gripping the fabric near my collar, kneading in a slow rhythm that matches his breathing. His left ear wiggles. His bandit mask of dark fur presses warm against the bare skin above my scrub top, and every few seconds his nose twitches, pulling in my scent like he's making sure I'm still here.

I am. I'm always here.

The small nursing bottle of formula sits empty on the desk behind me. It's his third feeding of the night. His intake is up, which is the good news. The bad news is that he screams like he's being murdered if the formula isn't delivered while he's pressed flat against my chest. Against skin. Specifically, against the soft, warm terrain between my breasts, or Maren's.

It's my own fault, but now here we are.

I learned this the hard way when I tried to transition to feeding him in his small cage like a reasonable medical professional. Ricky wobbled and tried to crawl toward me, shrieking with a volume that seemed impossible from a two-pound animal, until I scooped him up and pressed him against my breasts. Then silence. Then the frantic rooting of his nose against my shirt until it poked through the buttons and he found skin.

Then peace.

I'd looked down at his small gray and black body, his fur rising and falling with each contented breath, and the word that formed in my head was not a professional one.

Now it's been nineteen days, and the pattern is concrete. Ricky eats when he's held against a chest, sleeps when he's held against a chest, and exists in a state of relative calm only when pressed against the warm, yielding topography of a female torso. A female's boobs, to be exact. A distinction Maren has made at every available opportunity with a level of personal satisfaction that suggests she finds it the funniest thing that has ever happened in this building.

I shift him higher in the wrap as I move back to the sofa. I amputated two of his toes seventeen days ago. There was no saving them. His back paw is still tender, but he's improving. I can feel it in the way he repositions himself, the left hind leg bearing more weight now when he scrambles for a better grip. The antibiotics did their work, and his appetite is fierce. His eyes are bright, black as wet river stones, and full of calculating intelligence that makes me nervous.

He's going to be a problem. I can feel it in my bones.

But right now he's asleep, and my office smells like lavender from the candle burning on the desk, formula, and clean animal fur. I lean down to pet Shadow as I sink into the cushions, eyes closing. One minute is all I need. The world can wait that long.

I open them to daylight streaming in the window, and Maren's face six inches from mine.

"You drooled on him."

I blink and swallow. My neck is locked up because of the angle I slept in, and there's a line of dried saliva running from the corner of my mouth to Ricky's back. He doesn't seem to mind. He's awake, peering up at me and looking smug, his claws hooked into my scrub top right at the neckline, tugging it down.

"Stop that."

I unhook his claws from the fabric. He hooks them back in. I unhook them again. He tilts his head and hooks them in a third time, pulling the neckline lower.

"He's trying to see more boob," Maren says, and takes a sip from her coffee cup.

"He's nesting."

"He's nesting in your cleavage."

"He's seeking warmth and the sound of a heartbeat. It's a well-documented comfort behavior in orphaned mammals."

Maren raises one eyebrow, her dark curls heaped on top of her head. She looks like she got maybe six hours of sleep, which is two more than me.

"Luna. That raccoon has his entire face down your shirt. That's his default location these days."

I look down. Ricky has, in fact, worked his pointed snout under the edge of my top again and is pressing his nose into the curve of my left breast. His eyes are half-closed in what can only be described as bliss.

I extract him. He chitters in protest and reaches for my shirt with both paws.

Maren sets her mug on the side table and holds out her hands.

"Give him here. I need to do his vitals before morning rounds."

I peel his claws from my shirt one by one and hand him over. The second he settles against Maren's chest, he goes quiet. His nose works against the V-neck of her scrub top, pushing at the fabric, his little hand gripping her breast, and his small body relaxes into boneless contentment.

Maren looks at him. Then back at me.

"We've created a boob monster."

I want to argue, but I'm too tired, and Ricky's movements and position undermine every clinical term I might deploy in my defense.

I look around. "Did you let Shadow out?"

"Yeah. He was doing a pee dance at the front door when I came in."

I heave myself off the sofa and follow Maren down the hall, stopping in the bathroom to splash water on my face and brush my teeth before I knock someone out with my breath. Then I head outside.

The wolf enclosure is first. Shadow is lying in front of the gate as I approach, back from his usual morning run. I crouch beside him as he stands up.

"Hi, baby. I'm sorry I didn't wake up to let you out."

He headbutts my shoulder, rubbing his nose against my neck as he greets me. I scratch along his back the way he loves, and he lets out a contented growl as he looks at me with those intelligent eyes.

The ones that say, "I get it. You're exhausted."

I release a long breath. Peace settles in my chest. It always does with Shadow. With any wolves. It's a frequency I can't explain and stopped trying to a long time ago.

I breathe in the cool mountain air. For thirty seconds I'm just a woman in a beautiful place, and my body doesn't hurt, and my eyes don't burn, and I'm not thinking about formula schedules or wound care or the current grant application sitting unfinished on my desk.

Then my phone buzzes in my pocket.

Maren's voice comes through the second I answer it. "Luna, he's doing the thing again."

I close my eyes. "Which thing?"

"The screaming thing. I put him on the scale to weigh him, and he's doing his impression of a fire alarm."

Through the phone comes the piercing shriek of a raccoon who has been separated from his preferred resting place and finds this state of affairs unacceptable.

"I'm coming."

Maren is standing beside the exam table with her hands on her hips when I find her in the main medical area. Ricky's front paws scratch against the scale, mouth open, producing a sound that vibrates somewhere behind my back teeth. His dark eyes are locked on Maren with an intensity that borders on accusation.

"He weighs two point one pounds," she says over the noise. "Up from two yesterday. Temperature is normal. Foot looks good. He's thriving." She pauses. "He's also a tiny terrorist."

Ricky scrambles over the side of the scale's basket. The second my hand makes contact with his fur, the screaming stops. I lift him, and he scrambles up my chest and dives down the front of my shirt with a speed that makes me gasp. He settles between my breasts and nuzzles my skin and releases a long, rattling purr that I feel more than hear.

The silence is almost shocking.

"I rest my case," Maren says.

I get as far as drawing breath and stop there. There's nothing to say that the purring raccoon in my shirt hasn't already said for me.

⎯⎯⎯⎯◆⎯⎯⎯⎯

An hour later, I hand Ricky off to Maren again before heading over to the house to shower and change and grab something to eat. It sits about ten yards to the left of the main sanctuary building. It was my grandfather's house. The house he was raised in and the one I was raised in after my parents died.

I haven't been inside it for more than a quick shower and a change of clothes in days, and I feel like I've lived on protein bars for the last few weeks. I need something more substantial to eat.

I feed the girls first. They're furious with me. Juniper, my gray, fluffy, chunky, vocal girl, makes her annoyance at my absence known in no uncertain terms by biting my bare foot. Sage, my calico runt, climbs up my leg and settles on my lap, purring, her motor vibrating my thighs. Willow, my black-and-white cranky girl, jumps on the table and eyes me with the resentment only a cat who has been neglected for days can display.

It's happened before when I've had a neonatal animal to care for, but they don't care. They're still mad. I give them extra treats, and that seems to pacify them.

I call Shadow in and feed him before checking the fridge for something to eat. There's leftover chicken salad with grapes and walnuts that Maren made for dinner two nights ago. I make a sandwich and head back over to the main building to check on Tate. He's been cleaning Zorro's enclosure this morning.

I walk down the corridor that runs alongside the indoor habitats. Our resident adult raccoon has been watching us, sitting in the crook of his favorite oak branch, tracking every interaction with Ricky with an expression I can only describe as offended.

Raccoons don't do subtle.

Tate is inside when I reach it, moving through the habitat with a bucket and a scrub brush, working around the base of the artificial rock feature. Zorro is on his branch, grooming himself. I step inside with my sandwich in one hand, and Tate looks up from where he's scrubbing.

"How's the water feature drain?"

"Clear now. There was a—"

Tate's mouth stays open around the unfinished word, and I follow his gaze.

Zorro is no longer on his branch.

He's on the platform beside me, sitting upright, his dark eyes moving between my face and the sandwich in my hand with an intensity that should be a warning. I register what's happening one second too late. He reaches over with one black hand, holds my gaze, and lifts the sandwich clean out of my fingers.

Then he turns and walks back toward his oak branch. No rush. Tail high. The sandwich held out in front of him like a trophy he always knew was his. I knew I shouldn't have brought the sandwich in here.

"Did he—"

"Yes."

"While looking at you?"

"That's Zorro's whole thing. The eye contact is the point."

He settles on his branch, sandwich clutched to his chest, and begins dismantling the sourdough piece by piece. His tail puffs out a half-inch wider than normal, and one eye stays on us.

"I don't get it," Tate says.

"He knows."

"Knows what?"

"He's been in here alone for almost two years. Has every routine in this building memorized. Four weeks ago, a new raccoon arrived. Staff behavior changed, and everyone keeps looking toward his enclosure and then at each other." Zorro tears off a piece of bread and pops it into his mouth. "He's not stupid."

"So he's what? Upset?"

"Not upset. Pre-emptively annoyed. There's a difference."

Tate considers this with a smirk. "Is that a technical term?"

"It's an accurate one."

Zorro finishes the bread layer and starts on the chicken salad, pausing between bites without taking his eyes off us.

"So how do you deal with that?"

I sigh. "It's too early to introduce them, so we start with scent introduction through the mesh first. Visual exposure. We don't rush the timeline." Zorro picks a grape out and brings it to his mouth. "He'll come around. He's just registering his complaint through official channels."

The door opens behind us, and Maren steps in, Ricky's small masked face visible above the neckline of her shirt, his curious eyes alert, sweeping the enclosure, taking in the interesting new territory.

Zorro goes still on his branch. He looks at Ricky. Looks at the remnants of my sandwich. Then back at Ricky.

"Oh, he does not look happy," Tate says.

"He's processing."

"He looks like my dad when my mom told him we were getting another dog."

Maren points at Zorro as Ricky makes a small, questioning churr.

"Since when does Zorro eat my chicken salad?"

"He stole it from Luna while looking straight at her."

"Oh, snap."

Maren walks closer and holds up her hand to high-five Zorro. He looks at it, then lifts another scoop of chicken salad into his mouth as his eyes lock onto Ricky beneath her chin.

Ricky slaps his paws over his eyes, and he disappears back down her shirt.

"Maren, you should back up."

She does with slow steps, a grin spreading across her lips.

"He's a sandwich bandit."

She laughs at her own joke. Tate joins in.

"He's demonstrating resource awareness in response to perceived territorial—"

"Luna." Maren reaches into her collar and pulls Ricky's head out of her shirt with two fingers. He emerges blinking, then presses both paws over his eyes again. She turns him to face her, and he churrs against her neck. "He stole your sandwich. And looked at you while he did it. He's a passive-aggressive thief, and he deserves that sandwich for being so slick."

Zorro drops his crust off the branch. It hits the floor in front of Tate's foot. He looks down at it. Then up at Zorro, who sits with his hands folded against his belly, looking back with the infinite patience of an animal who has made his point.

"Okay," Tate says. "I think I get it."

I bend down and pick up the bread, handing it back to Zorro.

"I think it's clean enough in here, Tate. Scoop his litter boxes, and let's leave him to decompress. We have a while before we have to introduce them. He'll get there in his own time."

I exit through the door with Maren behind me. Ricky pokes his head out of Maren's shirt now that it's just the two of us, his eyes wide and full of that watchful curiosity that keeps me up at night.

Zorro watches him go from his branch.

"Those two are going to be a nightmare together," Maren says.

I look over my shoulder as Zorro examines the bread I handed back to him before throwing it at Tate's head.

"Hey."

"Yeah, we're in for trouble."

⸻

We spend the rest of the day the way we spend every day now, working the sanctuary with a raccoon strapped to someone's front. We trade him back and forth like a relay baton. The handoff is always the same. Careful extraction of tiny claws from fabric or skin, a brief moment of outraged chittering, then the instant relaxation when he finds new soft boobs to rest against.

By four in the afternoon, I'm sitting on the kitchen floor, mixing Zorro a bowl of plain yogurt, strawberries, and sunflower seeds. A peace offering after this morning's events. Ricky is asleep in the wrap, his paws twitching. Is he dreaming? What do raccoons even dream about? Trash, probably. Shiny things. The warm dark space between a woman's breasts.

Maren appears in the doorway and leans against the frame.

"So, I have to go to dinner tonight."

I look up from the bowl. "Dinner?"

"With Estella. My grandmother. You remember her? Short. Feisty. Curses like a sailor in Spanish, which is where I get it from. And convinced I'm going to hell for my life choices."

The guilt hits me before I can brace for it. "Shit, Mar, I'm sorry."

"No worries. She wanted me to bring you, but I told her we can't leave the pervert over there."

"Go." I don't hesitate. "I'll be fine. He goes almost five hours between feedings now. I can get some solid sleep in between. You don't need to stay up here anymore. Go see Estella, but take a shower first. There's something in your hair."

Maren reaches up and pulls a small tuft of raccoon fur from her curls. She examines it, then flicks it away. "You sure?"

"Yes. And give her a hug and kiss from me."

Maren gives me one last look before she turns and heads out, leaving me and Ricky in the kitchen.

Chapter Nine

Luna

I give Zorro his treat, and he stares at it like he's offended by the bribe, but not long after I leave his enclosure, I hear him eating, and relief floods me.

The early evening rounds pass without incident. The wolves are settled, the barn cats have fresh water and treats, and in the recovery den, the two owls that came in after some teenagers used them for target practice sit quiet in their cages. Ricky sleeps through all of it, his small body generating a heat against my chest that feels like coal wrapped in velvet.

By seven o'clock, the sanctuary is still, and the sky has gone purple over the peaks. I stand in the doorway of my office, looking at the sofa I've been sleeping on for the better part of a month, with its permanent dent in the middle cushion and the blanket that smells like raccoon and exhaustion. Ricky shifts against me, his eyes opening, staring up at me, and I make a decision.

"We're going to the house tonight, buddy. I've gotta feed the girls and Shadow anyway, but we're gonna stay there tonight."

I grab the formula supplies, the warming pad, and the small mesh playpen I use when I absolutely need both hands free. I load it all into a canvas bag, tuck Ricky tighter in the wrap, and exit the main building. Shadow lopes out of the tree line and falls into step beside me. His shoulder brushes my hip. I drop a hand to his head.

"Hi, baby. Did you have a good run?"

Maren's SUV still sits in front of the house. What the hell?

The smell hits me first when I reach the porch. Green chile, roasted onion, cumin, and underneath it, the warm corn-and-oil smell of tortillas.

I push open the front door, and the wall of warmth and smell hits me so hard my eyes sting. My stomach growls louder than Shadow when he perceives a threat. The lights are on in the living room, and a fire has been lit in the fireplace.

Rick Springfield's "Jessie's Girl" is at full volume from the iPod station on the mantel. Maren and her eighties music. I wait for a break between verses.

"Hello?"

I reach the kitchen and find two figures moving around, one small and compact, gesturing with a wooden spoon, the other one a little taller and much curvier, swatting the spoon away.

Maren is at the stove, looking into the oven at a baking dish of enchiladas. Beside her, barely reaching the counter, stands Estella Rodriguez.

She's four foot eleven, eighty years old, and has never once in her life been intimidated by anything. Her silver hair sits in a neat bun behind her head. Her reading glasses hang from a chain around her neck, resting against a small gold crucifix. She's wearing a pressed blouse, dark slacks, and an apron that says YOU'LL EAT IT AND YOU'LL LIKE IT, which Maren bought her as a joke and which Estella wears without irony because she believes they're words to live by.

"Mija!" She turns and opens her arms. Her keen eyes find me and then drop to the lump in the wrap against my chest. "Is that the little bebé?"

"Estella." My voice comes out thick. I clear my throat. "What are you doing here?"

"What does it look like I'm doing? I'm feeding you. Maren says you've both been eating granola bars for weeks, like animals yourselves. Sit down."

Maren catches my eye over Estella's head and gives me a look that is equal parts apology and satisfaction.

"She wouldn't take no for an answer. She said, and I quote, 'I'm not letting you come here and eat my enchiladas while Luna starves on that mountain like a goat.'"

"Like a goat," Estella confirms, pointing the spoon at me. "Sit."

I sink into the kitchen chair. Not because I'm told to. At least, that's what I tell myself, and the tight feeling I've been holding in my chest for twenty-five days loosens.

The girls come rushing in, dancing around my feet, looking for more treats, I'm sure. Estella approaches and peers into the wrap after pressing a kiss to the crown of my head. Ricky's black eyes blink up at her before he covers them with his little fingers.

"Pobrecito." Estella reaches out one weathered hand and touches his ear with a gentleness that contradicts every hard thing about her. "He's so small. And you carry him like that all day?"

"It's a therapeutic bonding wrap. He has attachment needs that require bodily contact for regulation of his nervous system."

"I told you he likes boobs, Abuela," Maren calls from the stove.

"Maren Lucia Rodriguez."

"What? It's true. That raccoon is more obsessed with tits than any guy I dated in college. And that's saying something, because Kyle Brennan once tried to—"

"Ay! I don't want to hear it." Estella crosses herself and looks at the ceiling. "Dios mio, give me strength."

Maren grins at me. I feel the corner of my mouth pull up for the first time in what feels like weeks.

The enchiladas come out of the oven golden and bubbling, stuffed with spinach and cheese and bathed in a green chile sauce that Estella makes from scratch. The recipe is her mother's, who brought it from Guadalajara, and Estella guards it like a state secret. Maren has been trying to steal it for years. She's gotten close twice, and both times Estella caught her snooping in the recipe box and chased her out of the kitchen with a rolled-up newspaper.

Maren sets three plates on the table. Then she pulls a pitcher from the counter and holds it up.

"You made margaritas?"

"Estella made margaritas. She brought her own tequila."

Estella shrugs. "You don't leave good tequila in an empty house."

The first sip of margarita on an empty stomach hits me like a tranquilizer dart. It slides down my throat and blooms warm in my belly, and my shoulders drop about three inches.

The enchiladas are perfect. They're always perfect, and Estella knows it. She sits across from me and watches me eat with her clear, level eyes that don't miss a thing. She's a woman who considers feeding people a sacred calling, and there is no neutral response to her cooking. Like her apron says, you eat and enjoy it, or you answer for it.

Ricky churrs and wriggles against my chest. His small hand reaches up from inside the wrap, and he pats my jaw, his claws just grazing skin. He bumps his nose into my neck more than nuzzles it, then tucks himself back down and goes to sleep.

"So." Estella sets her fork down. "When is the last time you went on a date?"

Maren groans. "Leave Luna alone."

"I'm asking a simple question. She's a beautiful woman living alone on a mountain with animals. It's not natural."

"You know what else isn't natural? Your obsession with our love lives. Luna, back me up."

I take another sip of my margarita and stay out of it. This is a conversation I've witnessed at least forty times. I know my role. I'm Switzerland.

"You're both thirty-two years old, mija." Estella locks her gaze on Maren. "You have a boyfriend who is never around. And he's not even a nice Catholic boy."

"Estella, don't start in on my man."

Estella shakes her head because the topic of JT never ends well. Her eyes find mine.

"And you. No boyfriend. No husband."

"Times have changed, Estella," I say, wading in even though I know I shouldn't.

"You know what hasn't changed? The fact that God intended for people to make families. Not live on a mountain covered in raccoon spit in the chest area."

"The boob region," Maren corrects. "You can say boobs, Estella. It's not a sin."

Estella points her fork at Maren. "This is why you can't find a good man. What man wants a woman who makes jokes about—"

"About what? Sex? Because I guarantee you, men love women who talk about sex. That's never been a problem for me."

Estella crosses herself again. "Por el amor de Dios."

"I'm just saying. My mouth has never been the issue. If anything, it's been a selling point."

I choke on my margarita. Maren catches my eye and winks.

Estella closes her eyes. Her lips move in what I'm fairly certain is a silent prayer. When she opens them, she looks at me.

"Luna. Talk some sense into her. You're the reasonable one."

"Don't drag me into this."

Estella sighs and turns her gaze back to Maren. "I only want what's best for you, mija. It's been twenty-eight years since your parents, those pedazos de mierda, dropped you off at my door."

I don't have to be fluent in Spanish to know that phrase. I've heard Estella say it enough times over the years. Maren's fork pauses over her plate.

I know the story. Everyone who loves Maren knows it. Estella's son, David, and his wife, Carmen, drove five-year-old Maren to Estella's house on a Tuesday night. They said they were going to see a movie and asked Estella to watch the girl for a couple of hours. She made Maren hot chocolate, and they watched cartoons together, and when the movie should have ended, no one came. When midnight rolled around, no one came. And when Tuesday became Wednesday and then Thursday and then a full week, Estella stopped waiting and started raising.

David and Carmen surfaced once, three years later. A phone call from somewhere in Texas. They wanted money. Estella told them where they could shove their request, and that was the last anyone heard from them.

Maren takes a gulp of her margarita. The loud, brash, unfiltered version of her that fills every room she walks into has pulled back behind her eyes, and for a few seconds there is a smaller, quieter person sitting in her chair. It always passes, but I've watched it happen enough times to stop pretending I don't.

I reach over and squeeze her thigh, and tension radiates through her jeans.

"Pedazos de mierda," Estella repeats, her voice flat and hard. Then she reaches across the table and covers Maren's hand with her own. Her face changes. The woman who was iron a moment ago is gone, and the grandmother underneath looks at Maren the way you look at the one person you would burn everything else down to protect. My throat tightens around nothing.

"But if they hadn't been, I wouldn't have had the gift of raising you." She lifts Maren's hand to her cheek and holds it there. "God works in mysterious ways."

The room is silent for a few seconds. Then Maren sets her glass down, and that quiet person is gone, tucked away again. My best friend is back, and she laughs. It's a real laugh, a Maren laugh.

"Did you just say God works through pieces of shit?"

"I said what I said."

Maren pulls Estella's hand to her lips and kisses her arthritic knuckles. "I'm pretty sure that's not in the Bible, Abuela."

"It should be. I'll write the Pope a letter."

I blink back the moisture in my eyes and refill everyone's margaritas. Ricky wakes up during the second round and demands to be fed, which I do at the table while Estella watches with a mixture of fascination and tenderness. He wraps both paws around the bottle and latches on, his eyes dropping to half-mast. Formula bubbles up at the corners of his mouth and spreads into a white mustache and beard. He looks like a tiny, milk-drunk professor.

"He thinks you're his mama," Estella says.

The words pull at the place in my chest where I keep the things I don't say out loud. I don't respond. I watch him eat and pretend I don't feel what I feel.

⸺◆⸺

The third round of margaritas is probably a mistake. The tequila is doing its work on all of us. Estella's cheeks are pink. Maren leans back in her chair with her feet up on the empty fourth seat, gesturing with her glass while she tells the story of the time Old Man Henderson's goat escaped and ate her bra off the clothesline.

"I'm just saying, this sanctuary has a thing for my chest. First the goat, now the raccoon. It's a pattern."

"You hung your bra outside like a flag," Estella says. "What did you expect?"

"I expected it to dry. Not become a goat snack."

I shake my head at the memory. "You should have seen how red Mr. Henderson's face got when he had to wrestle it away from Pip and hand what was left of it back to Maren."

"Pip?" Estella looks between us as her lips quirk.

"That's the name of Henderson's goat," Maren replies.

Ricky finishes his bottle and smacks his lips, a gesture so human it's almost disturbing, before he squirms against me. He's entering the post-feeding restless phase, where he needs to be burped and repositioned, or he gets fussy. He wriggles up my chest to my shoulder, gripping my hair for leverage. I pull his fingers away and pat his small back in slow circles until the burp comes out, half chirp, half belch. Before the sound has fully left him, he dives behind the wrap, rooting around against my shirt collar like he's after something buried in there.

"Hey. Knock that off."

I hold my shirt against my chest, and he changes course, finding a gap between two buttons further down. He shoves his face through it, his whiskers tickling my skin. I extract him and hold him at arm's length. He dangles there, all four limbs spread, and the look on his face is so aggrieved and so personal that I have to look away to keep a straight face.

Estella pats my arm. "At least someone wants to be close to you, mija. Since you won't find a man."

"Estella."

"I said what I said."

"Here." Maren laughs and holds out her hands to me. "My turn. You need to eat another enchilada, or that margarita is going to your head."

I pass him across the table. Maren tucks him against her chest. His nose finds the V of her shirt within three seconds. His paws press into the curve of her left breast, and he squeezes, his small body going limp with contentment as he settles into the warm space he's found.

Maren looks down at him and rubs her finger against his ear. "You know, you've got real confidence."

She heads for the bathroom. The faucet turns on, and then Ricky's indignant chirping comes over the sound of the water.

"Clean the sink when you're done."

"What am I? An amateur?"

I pull the enchilada plate closer and take another one, even though I'm not that hungry. But Maren is right. I'll wake up with a major hangover tomorrow unless I get something to soak up this tequila in my stomach. I need some water, too.

Estella refills her own glass from the blender. My lips curve. She catches me watching and shrugs. "What? I'm eighty. I've earned it."

Maren and Ricky return, his little pointed face sticking out of her collar as she sits. Willow chooses that moment to jump on the table. She's been watching from the windowsill for the past twenty minutes, her slender black and white body coiled tight. She stalks between the plates, ignoring Estella's startled "Ay," walking up to Maren and stretching her neck toward Ricky, sniffing.

Ricky's eyes snap open. He and Willow regard each other from six inches apart. Then he covers his eyes with his hands.

"Easy," I murmur, putting a hand on her back.

She hisses, but I keep my fingers on her spine. Ricky peeks out from behind his fingers, then squirms in Maren's shirt, both paws reaching toward Willow like he's decided they're friends. Maren grabs him by the scruff before he clears the collar. He chitters, outraged, legs still pedaling toward Willow like if he kicks hard enough, the rules will change, the opposite of his reaction to Zorro earlier.

Willow finishes her investigation on her own terms, pulling back with a look of pure feline disdain, then jumps down from the table and stalks to the corner, where she sits with her back to all of us.

Classic Willow.

"That one has an attitude," Estella observes.

"That one is my soulmate," Maren says, taking a sip of her margarita.

Sage, who has been purring on my lap this whole time, stretches and bumps her tiny calico head against my stomach before jumping down. She heads over to Shadow, lying by the kitchen door like a sphinx, and climbs onto his back.

Juni watches all of this from the chair beside me, her chunky gray body taking up the entire seat. I reach over and stroke along her back. She leans into it, eyes closing. I keep going. She leans more. I scratch behind her ears, and she tips her head. Then, with zero warning, she bites my finger.

"Ow, Juni."

She blinks at me and starts licking her paw.

"Your animals are insane," Maren says. "Every single one."

Shadow lifts his head.

"Except you, handsome." She blows him a kiss. "You're perfect."

He puts his head back down. He knows.

"I should let him out for his last run."

The cool air hits me as I open the kitchen door, and I breathe it in, letting it cut through the tequila fog. Shadow dislodges a protesting Sage and slips past me into the darkness without a sound. Seven years old and he's still the most beautiful thing I've ever seen.

He disappears into the treeline, a gray ghost swallowed by the trees. He'll run the perimeter, checking the boundary of his territory, making sure nothing has encroached while he's been inside tolerating house cats, half-drunk women, and a raccoon. Then he'll come back and sleep by my bed, or by the front door, or wherever he decides is the most strategic position to guard me from.

Maren pushes my glass toward me when I return to the table. She pulls Ricky out of her shirt and settles him on his back across her thighs. He kicks his arms and legs as she tickles his belly. He grabs her index finger with both hands and pulls it to his mouth.

"Oh, hey. Did I tell you what I heard from Eleanor yesterday when I was in town?"

Eleanor is Aspen Ridge's postmistress. Has been forever. She and her husband of fifty-four years, Frank, work there together, and she's the town gossip. If anything happens in Aspen Ridge, Eleanor knows about it. And as soon as she does, so does everyone else.

"What'd she say?"

"Someone's buying the Morrison estate."

Estella's hand stops midway to her glass. The kitchen goes quiet except for Sage's purring and the low hum of the refrigerator.

"Dios mío." Estella's hand goes to her crucifix. She crosses herself for the fourth time tonight. "That house. That terrible house."

I pick up my margarita and take a long sip. The Morrison property has been a dark spot on our little town. The house is visible from the eastern ridge trail and looks like it was built to hold secrets. People in town don't talk about it.

"You're kidding me. Who?"

"Some billionaire. Supposedly Denver's most eligible bachelor."

"A billionaire buying a serial killer's house in the middle of the mountains." I turn my glass in my hands. "That's not weird at all."

"Maybe they're going to tear it down," Estella says. "Build a nice, new family home."

"On five hundred acres bordering a wildlife sanctuary, with the nearest neighbor over a mile away?" Maren shakes her head. "That's not a family home buyer. That's someone who wants privacy."

Ricky has been eyeing Maren's chest for the last minute, and he goes for it, his fingers and good foot scrabbling against her stomach, the bum one splaying wide. She pulls him back down, and he protests with a short churr, but I'm pleased to see that foot has more push in it than it did last week.

"Or someone who likes the history," she adds, and a hushed silence falls over the room.

"You're going to give me nightmares," Estella says. "Change the subject."

"It's probably nothing," I say, more for Estella's benefit than because I believe it. "Rich people buy properties like that all the time. Flip them. Turn them into vacation rentals."

"A vacation rental in a murder house?" Maren says. "I'd book it."

"You're going to hell," Estella says, shaking her head, but the corner of her mouth gives her away.

Maren shrugs, and the kitchen door rattles. I let Shadow back inside, his fur damp with dew. He shakes once, sending a fine mist across the kitchen floor before he returns to his spot by the door. His eyes find me and hold, and I see the report in them. Perimeter clear and territory secure.

"Good boy." I crouch and press my forehead to his. He huffs warm air against my face. His fur smells like pine needles, cold earth, and something wild underneath that will never be tamed, no matter how many years he sleeps on my bedroom floor.

I settle back at the table, and Maren pours the last of the margaritas. The tequila is warm in my blood, and the enchiladas are heavy in my stomach. The house feels full in a way it hasn't felt in months. Years, maybe. The fullness of people who love you, sitting in your kitchen, refusing to let you starve on a mountain like a goat.

Ricky gets fussy again around nine. Maren sets him on the table, and he sways on unsteady legs. He noses at her balled-up napkin without much conviction, more interested in the smell of it than anything else before he loses his balance and sits down hard. Then his head swings toward the salsa bowl. I scoop him up before he can take a step in that direction. He gets his claws in my collar the second he's close enough and pulls himself up my chest like a little climber scaling a rock face, diving under my shirt before I can stop him.

"Unbelievable," Maren laughs. "He doesn't even pretend to be subtle."

"He's barely five weeks old."

"He's a prodigy. I love him."

Estella yawns behind her hand.

"You two are staying tonight, right? It's late. Don't drive home in the dark."

Maren looks at Estella. Estella looks at her margarita glass, which is empty, and nods.

"I'm not letting you drive down that mountain after three margaritas," she says, and that's that.

"Fine. JT's still out of town anyway." Maren pushes back from the table as Estella makes a low noise in her throat that reveals exactly what she thinks of him. She picks up Maren's margarita glass, downing the last of it as she stands.

"You have your meds with you, right?" Maren asks, and she nods again. "You can take my bed. I'll crash on the couch."

"Don't be silly, mija. I'm not kicking you out of your own bed. We share."

Maren pauses, and a slow, wicked grin spreads across her face.

"Well, well, well. Estella Maria Rodriguez. You'll be the first girl I've had in my bed since college."

"Maren Lucia Rodriguez."

Shit! They're both using full birth names.

"I mean, other than Luna, but she doesn't count. I've been sleeping with her for over a decade."

Estella stands, and her hand connects with the back of Maren's head in a swift, practiced smack. "Your grandfather said the same thing once. I married him anyway."

"Estella, you hussy. I knew I got it from somewhere."

Estella moves to smack her again, but Maren catches her hand and pulls her into a hug that Estella pretends to resist for one second before she melts into it. I watch them from the table, and the ache in my throat comes back.

We clean the kitchen together. Maren washes, Estella dries, and I supervise from the chair because every time I try to stand, Ricky protests the shift with a series of chirps that make Estella flinch.

I hand him to Maren so I can deal with the leftovers. By the time the kitchen is clean, she passes him back to me for the last time. He doesn't open his eyes, claws finding my shirt by instinct, and noses his way under the fabric and down until he's pressed flat against me, his body curled between my breasts like he was made to fit there. His paws grip the soft flesh through the fabric of my bra with a possessive certainty that is, I have to admit, a little alarming. The churring starts back up, his whole body going slack against mine.

I look up to find Estella watching us from the doorway, a half-drunk smile curving her lips. She points one finger at the lump under my shirt.

"That animal is going to grow up to be completely obsessed with chichis."

"Estella!" Maren snorts.

"I said what I said."

The corner of my mouth pulls up. Fifteen years of knowing this woman, and that phrase has never once changed.

Estella turns and heads down the hallway toward the stairs. "Buenas noches, mijas. And for God's sake, put that raccoon in a cage before he puts his face somewhere that requires a confession."

Maren follows her, laughing. They walk upstairs, and Estella's voice rises and falls in her usual combination of English and Spanish, Maren's low chuckle threading through it. A door closes. Muffled conversation bleeds through the walls, then fades to silence.

I look down at Ricky. His mask of dark fur is pushed against my chest, and his breathing has gone shallow and even, his sides barely moving. Each tiny exhale brushes my skin, and his paws have loosened their grip. He's gone to wherever five-week-old raccoons go when the night is done with them.

"I'm gonna regret letting you do this, aren't I?"

He nuzzles closer, his nose pushing deeper into the curve of my breast, and sighs the long, contented sigh of a creature who has found where he belongs.

Chapter Ten

Damien

Thirty days, to the day after I first saw the Morrison Estate, I head north in the Range Rover. Jack Hadley, my architect, rides shotgun with a file folder balanced on his knees, flipping through historical photographs of the Morrison estate that his research assistant pulled from the county archives. Genevieve Parker, the interior designer I poached from a firm in Aspen last year, occupies the back seat with her iPad.

"The foundation is solid," Jack says, holding up a structural survey. "Which is miraculous for a house built in 1892. But the electrical is knob and tube throughout. The plumbing is original cast iron, and some of it has been patched with what looks like, and I'm not exaggerating here, actual lead solder."

"So we replace it."

"The house isn't on the National Register, which means we have more flexibility, but the exterior materials are going to take time to source if we want to honor what was originally there."

"Then we start with the interior."

Jack glances at me. He's worked with me long enough to recognize when a conversation is over before it's begun, but he's also an architect, which means he's incapable of not voicing his concerns.

"Even interior work has complications. Load-bearing walls, original millwork, plaster versus drywall considerations."

"Jack."

"Yes?"

"What's the number that would make you stop talking about complications and start talking about solutions?"

He pauses. I can see the gears turning behind his eyes, the mental spreadsheet expanding in real time as he factors in historical consultants, specialized craftsmen, expedited permits, and premium materials.

"Eight figures. Comfortably."

"Then be comfortable."

Genevieve leans forward from the back seat. "What are your priorities? If we're starting interior, I need to know which rooms take precedence."

"Master suite first. Bedroom, bathroom, walk-in. I want it livable within eight weeks. After that, the study on the main floor."

"Livable as in functional, or livable as in finished?"

"As in I should be able to sleep, shower, and work without thinking about the fact that I'm in a construction zone. Whatever that requires."

Jack glances over at me. "Damien, that kind of timeline is not—"

"Eight figures, Jack. Make it work. You have carte blanche to spend whatever is necessary to meet my timeline."

Genevieve makes a note on her iPad. "Bathroom will need full plumbing. New fixtures, new lines throughout the entire house. And if you want your usual tech setup in the study, we're going to need to run fiber. There's no existing infrastructure for that kind of connectivity up here."

"I'll start with satellite service, but we'll need to trench it in eventually. Get the applications started, and I'll reach out to the governor and get approval to run the line up from Estes myself."

Jack raises an eyebrow. "You're talking millions in additional expenses."

I glance at him but don't reply.

We pull into the driveway, and the house rises through the trees like a beast surfacing from deep water. I park, and for a moment, none of us move.

"Jesus," Genevieve breathes. "It's even more majestic than the pictures. But, shit, it's in rough shape."

"That's why I have you two."

I take them through the front door, and I swear I hear Jack whimper. I knew this would give him a hard-on. It's an architect's and designer's dream project.

I lead them upstairs to the master bedroom first. It occupies the entire north wing of the second floor, with views of the mountains through bay windows. The attached room, which was once a dressing chamber, will become the new bathroom.

"I want a walk-in rain shower. Double vanity. Heated floors. Knock out this wall to expand the bathroom footprint. The closet can take the space from the adjacent bedroom. I don't need seven of them."

Jack moves through the room with his laser tool, clicking off measurements at each wall. Genevieve follows a step behind him with her camera, murmuring to herself about tile and fixture finishes, already deep inside a version of the room that doesn't exist yet.

We head downstairs to the study. It's wood-paneled with built-in shelving running floor to ceiling on two walls and a stone fireplace anchoring the corner. I press my palm flat against the shelf. Behind it, through perhaps twelve inches of plaster and lathe and old timber, sits the formal dining room. A room I have no use for. Not as a dining room, anyway.

"I want a concealed door here." I tap the bookshelf. "Behind this unit. The shelves swing open on a hinge. Magnetic latch, no visible hardware. Behind it, I want the formal dining room converted into a private room."

Jack and Genevieve exchange a look.

"The formal dining room is one of the most architecturally significant spaces in the house," Jack says. "The original plaster medallion on the ceiling, the wainscoting, and the built-in china cabinet. They're referenced in three separate historical surveys."

"There are two dining rooms."

"The other one is considerably smaller. More of a breakfast room."

"It's a dining room now. Move the medallion and china cabinet if you're so worried about them."

"Damien, I have to advise against this. The formal dining room is a centerpiece of the original floor plan."

"Jack, I want a sealed, private room. No windows. The only access point is through the concealed door from this room. Can you do that?"

Jack pulls in a breath, holds it, and releases it through his nose. Then he nods. The answer is always yes when the budget is unlimited.

"What's the room for?" Genevieve asks. It's a reasonable question. She needs to know how to design it.

"Private collection." I meet her eyes. "I'll handle the interior myself. I just need the shell. Walls, climate control, fire suppression, lighting on a dimmer and motion sensor, and the concealed entry. Nothing else."

She writes it down and moves on. We finish the walkthrough, and I send them both back down the mountain with a timeline that Jack calls aggressive and I call necessary. The Range Rover disappears down the drive, and I go back inside.

Alone.

The air temperature drops as I descend the basement stairs. It's the first time I've been back since the day I toured it a month ago. I glance up at the exposed floor joists overhead. They don't look sturdy enough for the chains I plan to hang from them.

I call Jack and walk him through the structural replacement. The plumbing, heating, and electrical rough-in go on the priority list, same as the basement access before I seal it. Every contractor, inspector, or person with a clipboard and a reason will get their access now and never again. He murmurs his agreement and, for once, asks no questions he's not paid to ask.

I run my hands along the metal table and rickety wooden bench that I insisted to Elise I would dispose of myself.

The screams of the girls Morrison tortured and killed seem to linger down here, caught in the silence. He was a monster. They deserved so much better than the fate he gave them. They deserved to die in their beds, at ninety, surrounded by people who loved them. Unlike the men or women I'll bring into this room.

The ones I drag down here will deserve every second of their torment.

The front door opens upstairs, and I glance at my watch, surprised to see that two hours have passed. Heavy footsteps cross the foyer, pause, then move toward the hallway.

"Down here."

The basement door creaks open, and Cade's boots appear before he does. He stops at the bottom step as he scans the space the way he scans every space he enters—entry points, exits, sight lines, and vulnerabilities. He won't find any here.

"Well?" I gesture to the room.

He walks the perimeter, running his hand along the walls. He stops under the window and turns in a slow circle, hands in his pockets.

"It's perfect. Stone walls. One entry point." He moves to the drain and stands over it. "This is a gift. You get soundproofing down here and the right sealant on these floors. Cleanup is twenty minutes. Thirty if it gets messy."

"It'll get messy."

He looks at me. His face gives nothing away, but I've been reading Cade's reactions for twenty-five years. He's satisfied. This is better than the warehouse. The warehouse works, but it's always been a compromise. Too close to the city, too many variables, and too many cameras on the surrounding buildings that we have to account for every single time.

"Timeline?"

"Couple months. Maybe less if I keep the pressure on. Jack expects a lot of permitting red tape. It's going to require wining and dining the governor."

Cade nods. "That's your specialty."

"Fuck you."

"So, we'll keep using the warehouse until then."

"Yes."

We head upstairs and out the front door. The mountain air hits my lungs hard, nothing like the stale, heavy atmosphere below. We take Cade's truck down the mountain toward town.

Aspen Ridge is the kind of place that barely qualifies as a town, but there's something welcoming about it, even for me. It's a place where everyone knows everyone and strangers get noticed, which is why we need to become familiar faces. Unremarkable. The rich guy from Denver who bought the old Morrison place and his associate. Nothing more.

Nancy's Diner sits on the corner of Main and Elk. Inside, it's warm and smells like fresh coffee and apple pie. Red vinyl booths line the windows. A counter with swivel stools runs the length of the kitchen pass-through. Every surface is worn but clean, polished by decades of elbows and coffee cups and small-town conversation.

A woman with gray hair and glasses perched on her head waves us toward a booth.

"Sit anywhere, boys. Menus are on the table. Specials are on the board."

We slide into a booth by the window. Cade picks up the laminated menu and studies it with the same intensity he brings to surveillance dossiers. I scan it once. A young, red-haired waitress, with a name tag that says "Becca," comes over.

"What can I get you?"

"Bacon cheeseburger. Medium rare. Fries. Black coffee."

Cade orders the same without the bacon and adds a side of coleslaw, which is the most unsettling thing I've witnessed today, and I spent the morning standing in my new kill room.

Three men in flannel shirts fill the booth behind Cade. Their conversation is the ambient noise of small-town, mountain life. Weather, spring turkey hunting season, and someone's truck transmission.

"Saw Dr. Foster at the feed store yesterday. She ordered another two tons of raw meat for those wolves of hers. Two tons. Every month."

My hand stills on my coffee cup as the second man shakes his head.

"My wife dragged me up to that sanctuary for their open house last fall. I'm telling you, she walked right into the enclosure with a wolf the size of a damn pony, and it rolled over like a golden retriever. Just showed her its belly."

"That's why they call her the wolf whisperer." The third man has a voice that sounds like it was never young.

Across the table, Cade's eyes find mine.

"She'd make a dead man look twice," the first man chimes in again. "Complete waste though. She'd rather share a bed with her wolf than any man in this town."

"She's got that feisty brunette working with her," the second one says. "The one with the curves and the tits."

"I didn't know you were into big girls."

"I wasn't until I stood behind her at the post office. Now all I can see is her bent over and that ass—"

"Earl Pruit." The older woman, who must be Nancy, stops by the table. "If I hear you talking about Maren like that again, I will ban you from my diner. Do you hear me? Have some respect. No wonder your wife left you and took your kids to Nebraska."

Cade's face darkens. He has a particular dislike for men who disrespect women. We both do, but for him, it's more than irritation. Maybe because he has a daughter. Who knows? But he looks like he wants to punch Earl in the face.

The burgers arrive, and I take a bite, and for a moment I forget about everything else because it is, without exaggeration, one of the best burgers I've ever eaten.

"This is delicious."

Cade chews and nods but says nothing. The highest compliment Cade gives food is silence.

The men behind us leave, but the name stays with me. *The wolf whisperer.* A woman who rehabilitates predators on the property that borders mine.

"An animal sanctuary is a perfect neighbor." I keep my voice low and neutral.

Cade looks up from his plate. "Could be a complication. Volunteers. Visitors. People coming and going on the adjacent property."

"It's a wildlife sanctuary, not a shopping mall. And there's no line of sight."

Cade leans back in his seat before picking up a fry and eating it, which is his way of conceding the point.

I don't mention the rest of it. Not the image forming in my mind of a woman who walks into a wolf enclosure and earns the submission of an apex predator that doesn't usually give it. And not what it does to me, the idea of a woman who collects broken, dangerous things and gives her life to putting them back together. That I keep to myself. It has no business being part of this conversation.

I file it away, leave a seventy-dollar tip on a thirty-dollar check, and we drive back up the mountain. While we were at the diner, my assistant, Tiffany, had another one of my Range Rovers delivered to the property.

Cade heads out in his truck not long after. I stand on the front porch of my new home as the sound of his engine fades down the drive and the silence of the mountain surrounds me.

The sun is dropping behind the western ridge. Beyond the dense wall of oak, aspen, and pine that marks the boundary of my property sits my closest neighbor. I can't see a single structure, fence line, or clearing through the trees. Nothing but timber and an unbroken expanse of forest and shadow.

But I know it's there. And somewhere inside it, a woman is walking among wolves.

How ironic is that?

Chapter Eleven

Maren

The thing about working at a wildlife sanctuary is that eventually, no matter how many degrees you have or how many years you've spent studying animal behavior, some furry little bastard is going to make you question every life choice you've ever made while copping a feel.

It's been almost three months since that limping, scheming, pervy little black-masked baby menace came into our lives, and I have the scratch marks on my cleavage to prove it.

I lean against the front porch railing and watch Luna sitting on the steps with a dish of blueberries, talking to Ricky in that low, honey-warm voice she reserves for the animals she loves most. Which, at this point, is all of them. The woman has never met a creature she couldn't pour her whole heart into, and that includes me, which is the reason I'm standing here at seven fifteen in the morning when I could be in bed with JT or my vibrator or both.

"You're staring at him like he's a baby."

"He is a baby." She hands him another blueberry, which he puts into his mouth before looking up at her for another one.

"He's almost a teenager in raccoon years who tried to unhook my sports bra yesterday."

Luna doesn't look up, but her shoulders shake.

"He was exploring."

"Riiight." I push off the railing and drop onto the step above them. "That's what JT says too. For the record, Ricky has better technique."

It's one of those early summer Colorado mornings, the kind that makes people buy property they can't afford. The mountains, the wildflowers, and the sky, a deep shade of blue that doesn't exist anywhere else and that every tourist loses their mind over. Somewhere out there, one of them is pulling over to take a photo to post with an inspirational quote on Instagram. For me, it means my hair has expanded to three times its normal volume, and I'll be sweating through my shirt by noon.

I drag a curl off my cheek where it's stuck as Luna passes me the blueberry dish and leans back, palms flat on the porch boards behind her. Those hazel-green eyes of hers are bright, and she's wearing that glow she gets when an animal is turning a corner.

Ten weeks ago, Ricky came to us, life hanging by a thread. Now he scampers around with actual purpose, that slight hitch in his gait from losing those two toes smoothing out more each day. He looks like a real raccoon now, a fluffy, silver-tipped furball with a black mask of cuteness engineered to make it impossible to stay mad at him. Even when he's being a complete degenerate.

I shift sideways as his little paw makes a grab for my left boob.

"So today's the big day."

Luna exhales. "Today's the day."

"You really think the official introduction of Señor Tits McGee to Zorro is gonna go well?"

"Can you please not call him that?"

Ricky climbs onto my knee, reaching for the bowl. I hand him another blueberry.

"Which one? Señor Tits McGee or Zorro?"

"Maren."

"What? Zorro is a dignified name for a raccoon. Very on-brand. Very Antonio Banderas."

She reaches over and pinches my thigh. Ricky grabs for her fingers, falling off my leg and hitting the porch with a soft thud.

"I meant the other one."

"Fine. Ricardo. Is that better? Deeply respectful of the raccoon who shoved his entire face down my shirt the second I walked through the door this morning, like he was searching for the meaning of life between my Double Ds."

Luna bites her lip. She's fighting it. She always fights it because she has this idea that laughing at Ricky's antics makes her a bad rehabilitator, which is insane. I've known this woman since we were both freshmen at CSU Fort Collins, sharing a dorm room that smelled like wet dog and instant ramen. Behind that earnest, soft-spoken, yet steely exterior lives someone who once snort-laughed so hard at a dick joke that she aspirated a piece of popcorn.

I flick a blueberry across the wood. Ricky rolls over and scampers after it, shoving it into his mouth.

"The introduction needs to go well." Luna stands, brushing dirt off her butt. "They're going to be sharing the enclosure. Zorro has been watching Ricky like he's deciding whether or not to swat him across the face with a glove."

"Should we get them little swords? Have them face off at dawn?"

"Don't joke about this. I'm worried, Mar. Zorro's an adult male who's had that habitat to himself for two years. He's always lived alone, even before he came to us, and now we're dropping a juvenile raccoon into his living room."

I look down. Ricky is flat on his back, foot pulled up to his mouth, chewing on it without a care.

"You have nothing to worry about. Zorro doesn't have tits. Ricky will have zero interest in harassing him."

"Maren. Be serious."

"I am serious. Serious about the fact that you have me here at the ass crack of dawn as a human shield because you know the second you set him on a branch, instead of climbing it like a normal raccoon, he's going straight for your boobs."

Luna opens her mouth, then snaps it shut.

"That's what I thought."

Here's the thing about me and Luna. People look at us and think they've got us figured out in about forty-five seconds. She's the quiet one, the gentle one, the woman who whispers to wolves and cries when she releases a rescue back into the wild. I'm the loud one, the crass one, the friend who says out loud what everyone else is thinking but won't say because they have social skills. And sure, that's not inaccurate. But it's only the first layer. The part underneath is more complex, and most people don't bother to look deeper.

Luna is the strongest person I know. Not strong like me. Not loud strong. Not "I'll-fight-you-in-a-parking-lot" strong. She's strong like bedrock. Like the roots of the ponderosas holding this entire mountain together. She built this sanctuary from nothing. Grief and the money her grandpa left her, from grant applications written at two in the morning, years of thankless volunteer work, and a stubbornness so quiet you don't even clock it until you try to move her and discover she's planted.

And me. For all my noise, I'm the one who falls apart in private. I'm the one who cried in the supply closet last month when we lost that red fox, the one with the broken femur, hit by a tourist more interested in making it to the trailhead before the good light went. He'd been making such good progress until he wasn't. Luna found me in there, of course. She always finds me. She sat down on an overturned bucket and pulled my head to her chest and didn't say one word because she knows that sometimes words aren't what a person needs. Sometimes what they need is to be held by someone who won't ask them to explain why they're broken.

That's us. She holds me together in private, and I make sure nobody takes advantage of the fact that she'd give her last breath to a dying animal and forget to save one for herself.

"Okay." Luna rolls her shoulders, and her voice shifts into the one that means the morning warm-up is officially over. "Here's the plan. I carry Ricky in. You're already inside with grapes, trying to entice Zorro to be nice and encourage Ricky to want to interact. We let Zorro set the pace. If he shows any stress signals, flattened ears, piloerection, teeth. We pull Ricky out and go back to parallel exposure through the mesh."

I push to my feet. "Ricky likes Cheetos. If we want to bribe him, I should have Cheetos."

The words are barely out before Luna looks up from Ricky and stares at me.

"Since when does he eat Cheetos?"

Fuck!

That was between me and Ricky. A private agreement with a raccoon. And I blew it because my mouth works like a hooker on Colfax Avenue in downtown Denver, open before anyone's finished negotiating the terms.

Luna's eyes narrow. "Maren."

Ricky looks up at me, and I swear if he could talk, he'd say, "Nice going, ding dong."

"Uh…" Luna's arms cross, and she waits. "I had Cheetos with my lunch on Monday. He grabbed one. I had to share, Luna. Look at that face. You can't eat Cheetos in front of that face and not share. That's not a thing a person can do."

"The dye is terrible for him."

"And yet…"

I gesture at Ricky, who is alive and thriving and attempting to scale my leg from the ankle up.

"It's terrible for you too."

"Says the woman who eats Doritos for breakfast when she's hungover. Same exact dye, by the way. I checked the label."

"Were you hungover on Monday?"

My mouth curves. "Depends on the kind of hungover you mean."

"Never mind. I don't want to know."

She does want to know. She always wants to know, and then immediately regrets it.

"Back to the introduction. Grapes are fine. If Ricky tries anything, redirect with the grapes."

"You want me to redirect a boob-obsessed raccoon with fruit."

"It's worked before."

Ricky is at my knee now, making real progress.

"It has never worked. Last Friday, he used his oatmeal dish as a launch pad to get at my chest."

Luna gives me the look she's been giving me since we were nineteen, and it still works as well as it did then. I've never developed immunity to.

"Fine. Grapes. And no tit jokes during the introduction."

"Thank you."

She peels Ricky off my pants and tucks him against her chest. He burrows his face into the curve of her neck and stays there. He's not digging at her collar, rooting around, or trying to grab her boobs. Luna runs a thumb along his spine, and he doesn't lift his head. Instead, he presses into her and holds on. He knows something is going down.

I fall into step behind them, reaching over Luna's shoulder to scratch under his chin with one fingernail. He chitters, and Luna laughs as his nose presses against the side of her neck.

Tate stands at the supply shelves in the recovery den when we pass through, clipboard under one arm, glasses sitting crooked on his nose like they always do. He's the kind of guy who has no idea what a nerdy hottie he is, but half the female volunteers are crushing on him. He lifts his head and takes one look at me, a half-step behind Luna like a shadow she didn't ask for, and turns back to the shelf.

I detour into the kitchen and grab the bowl of grapes from the fridge and meet Luna outside Zorro's cage. Calling it a cage is habit, the way you call a ranch house a cabin because that's what it was before the additions went on. It's not a cage. It's eighty square feet of layered habitat, climbing structures built from actual logs, living ferns along the base, and a shallow water feature in the corner that Zorro uses for washing his food like the discerning gentleman he is. The kind of place that costs more per square foot than my first apartment.

Zorro came to us two years ago from a family out in Cheyenne Wells on the eastern plains. They'd found him as a kit, and for a while he'd been everything they wanted. Small enough to cradle, curious enough to be entertaining, and strange enough to show off. Then he'd grown into his hands and his cleverness and his temper, and the novelty had curdled into inconvenience. They'd kept him, but keeping wasn't the same as caring. By the time he came to us, he'd spent two years in a barn tack room with a latched door, fed and watered but largely forgotten.

It's why I spend at least an hour every day I'm here hanging out in the enclosure with him.

When he arrived, he flinched at hands and stress-ate everything within reach, which is how he became the substantial fellow he is today. We've tried to manage his diet. It never sticks. He has a face that makes you give him second and sometimes third helpings, and not one of us has the spine to hold the line. It's like Juni. She's built the same way I am, all curves and substance, but we both know we're fabulous.

For the past month, Zorro has been parking himself at the mesh wall between his enclosure and the recovery den, his hands wrapped around the wire, his eyes on Ricky, wearing the expression of a creature who can see a problem rolling toward him and hasn't decided how to feel about it yet.

I slip inside first, grape bowl in hand, and move to the back wall. Zorro is on his log, the thick section of pine that runs up the right side of the enclosure and tops out near the ceiling. He tracks me with his eyes, and I hand him a couple of grapes, which he takes and gobbles down as I scratch behind his ears.

"Hello, handsome."

The door opens behind me. Luna carries Ricky in, and every muscle in Zorro's body switches on.

He doesn't retreat or posture. He goes still.

Luna crouches and sets Ricky at the base of the log. He grips the bark with both hands and looks up. Zorro looks down from his perch. Two raccoons on opposite ends of a pine log.

Ricky starts to climb. He usually moves like something fired from a launcher, all velocity and no planning, but right now he's taking his time, testing each step, his left hind leg working a little harder than the right. He makes it to the wide middle platform next to where I'm standing and stops.

He looks at Zorro. Then he looks at me. Then his eyes drop to my chest.

"Ricky."

He chitters.

"I'm warning you, perv. You blow this introduction because you can't keep your hands to yourself, and I'm putting you in a onesie."

Luna moves along the wall toward Zorro, keeping her body sideways. She reaches up and runs her hand along his back, giving him a long, slow stroke, and his posture shifts, the tension releasing one degree at a time. She murmurs to him, and I can't make out the words, but the tone is the same one she uses for all of them, the voice that says you're safe and I have you and nothing bad is going to happen here.

Zorro chitters at her, short and pointed, the raccoon equivalent of I'd like to file a formal complaint about the interloper in my living room.

"I know," she says. "This is your space, but wouldn't it be nice to have a friend?"

Of course she'd ask a raccoon if he wants a friend. God, I love this woman.

She steps back. Zorro's masked face turns toward Ricky.

I hold another grape out to him. He leans forward from his branch, grabs it from my fingers, and eats it without taking his eyes off the small raccoon below him.

I offer one to Ricky, my hand far enough away that he has to move forward to reach it. He does. One step, then another.

Zorro growls for the first time.

"Hey, now," I say, handing him another grape. "We're being civilized today."

Ricky is motionless on the platform. His hands grip the bark. His eyes lock onto Zorro. The whole enclosure goes quiet except for the water feature trickling in the corner and the sound of my own pulse in my ears.

This is the pause Luna builds every introduction around. The moment before two animals decide what they are to each other, the ancient language of territory and threat, and the possibility that neither of those things has to apply here.

Zorro takes one cautious step along the branch, his thick tail held straight out behind him. He's enormous next to Ricky. Ricky is a stuffed animal someone left on a log. Zorro is an actual adult raccoon who weighs as much as a small dog and could end this introduction in a way nobody wants, but under all that chittering and suspicion, he's curious.

Ricky sits back on his haunches and looks at Zorro. Luna edges around me, moving closer to him in case this goes south. And her shirt moves.

Ricky's head snaps toward her chest like a compass needle finding north.

"Ricky, no—"

He launches.

Five pounds of raccoon become airborne, aimed with total commitment at Luna's chest. She catches him the way you catch a thing you didn't see coming, which is to say she absorbs the impact with her whole body and immediately starts losing the fight. He's up her front before she can get a proper grip, those dexterous little hands moving, back feet scrabbling against her stomach. His hands go for the collar of her shirt, and Luna stumbles backward, trying to get hold of him without squeezing, because you don't squeeze a baby raccoon, and the trying-not-to-squeeze problem is her downfall.

Zorro retreats to the highest branch and watches from there, which is the most intelligent decision anyone in this enclosure has made in the last thirty seconds.

"Maren, help—"

I drop the grapes and lunge, both hands snatching Ricky around the middle, but my vision blurs because I'm laughing so hard I can barely see. Luna's feet go first. The rest of her follows with a flat crack against the tile, her shirt bunched sideways, and hair fanned over her face like she's been tossed there.

"Oomph."

She lies still, mouth open, the impact having knocked the wind out of her.

Ricky twists in my grip, one hand grasping for my collar as the other reaches, with unmistakable intent, toward my left breast.

"Oh no, you don't."

I hold him at arm's length. He hangs there, looks at my face, drops his eyes to my chest, and looks back at my face. The unself-conscious audacity of it stops my laughing. Honestly. The consistency. You have to respect it a little.

Luna is sprawled on the floor, her shoulders jerking, her chest hitching, and every time she gets close to catching her breath, a snort escapes her and sets her off again. She covers her face with both hands, but the snorts keep coming anyway.

I drop down beside her, and the laughter hits me again. Ricky seizes the opening. He crawls up my front, tucks his face against my neck, and gets a fist around my left breast and squeezes.

I let him. After those acrobatics, he's earned some boob action.

The door swings open, and Tate leans through.

"Everything okay back here?"

It sets us off again. I press my hand over my face as tears run into my hairline.

"Alright then. I'll go back to my—"

Tate backs out the door.

Ricky lifts his head, surveys the situation, and then dismounts from my chest and scurries the three feet to Luna. He climbs onto her, turns in a small circle, and settles with his chin resting between her boobs with a sigh.

Luna places her hand on his back and stares up at the ceiling, still trying to catch her breath.

Warm fingers press against my left hand.

Zorro's on the floor beside me, one paw resting against my fingers, moving with gentle strokes. His other one holds a grape he retrieved from the floor somewhere. He chews and watches Luna and Ricky, his fingers never stopping their slow passes against my fingers.

I pick up another grape from the floor between us and hand it to him before rubbing his belly. His churring starts low in his chest and works its way through his body and into my palm.

His warm weight settles against my hip. I scratch behind his ears again, and he leans into my hand.

He watches Ricky the way you watch a television show you didn't choose but find yourself pulled into anyway. Interested, not ready to commit to anything yet, but not going anywhere either.

Maybe the meet and greet didn't go so bad after all.

Chapter Twelve

Maren

The morning is warm, and the porch swing moves in that lazy back-and-forth motion that makes it hard to justify getting up. Ricky's got his face tucked into my collar and both paws planted on my chest like Velcro, which is what mornings look like now. We don't carry him around in the wrap much anymore, only breaking it out on days he's clingy. He's big enough and more interested in chaos and independent destruction to want to be carried all the time. Thank fuck! But that still doesn't stop him from treating every woman on this property as a personal groping opportunity, especially me and Luna.

I let him have this morning's swing session because the alternative is to get up and start working, and I'm not there yet.

I spent the night because JT is on a run to California, and it was Chinese food Wednesday. Luna and I ate too much orange chicken and veggie lo mein and drank too much wine, and there was no way in hell I was getting behind the wheel.

As my hungover mind is imagining a nice, peaceful day at the sanctuary, Roger's truck pulls up the gravel drive at eight in the morning.

Well, shit. That's never a good sign.

Luna's front door opens, and she comes out, looking as good as I feel, Shadow trotting behind her.

She's down the steps and at Roger's door before I can set my coffee aside, hike Ricky over my shoulder, and follow.

"Family of four." He sets the crate on the tailgate. "Mom and three kits. Property outside Masonville. Guy was raising them in a chicken wire pen in his garage."

Luna crouches. Through the grates of the carrier, four pairs of black eyes catch the early light. The smell hits me a half-second later. It's not the spray or the full chemical weapon that skunks are famous for. This is the sour, yeasty stink of animals kept in their own waste, layered over unwashed fur and the metallic tang of stress.

Ricky squirms in my grip, eager to either escape the smell or investigate our new arrivals. I'm betting on the second one. He has no sense of self-preservation.

"How long did he have them?" Luna's voice has gone flat.

"Neighbors say since before the kits were born. He was selling them online."

Luna lifts the crate and carries it toward the building without another word. I grab Roger's arm before he can follow.

"How bad?"

"The mom's got sores on her feet from the wire floor. Kits are underweight, maybe half what they should be. One of them has an eye that doesn't look right."

"The guy?"

"Sheriff Mills came out. Cited. Three hundred dollar fine."

Three hundred dollars. The cost of a decent dinner for two in Denver. The cost of the life this man imposed on four living creatures who didn't ask for a chicken wire prison in a garage in Masonville.

The crate is on the exam table when I push through the treatment room door, and Luna is halfway into her coveralls, one arm in and one arm wrestling with the neck seal, her hair caught under the collar.

Ethan is here today, and he appears from wherever he goes when he's not being summoned by our crises. I deposit Ricky in his and Zorro's enclosure as he chitters in indignant protest and head back into the main treatment area.

Skunks don't let you cut corners on PPE. Leather gauntlet gloves that go to the elbow. Protective eyewear, N95 masks, and full disposable plastic coveralls that make the three of us look like a hazmat team that took a wrong turn.

We stand around the crate in our full ridiculous regalia and look at what Roger brought us.

The mother skunk is pressed into the far corner, her body curled over her three kits in a posture so old and so universal that it makes my heart hurt. She's thin, too thin, like she's not only missed a few meals but has also been feeding three babies and getting nothing back. Her black and white fur is matted, dull, and missing in patches along her back legs. The kits underneath her are tiny and trembling.

Luna loads a pole syringe with the sedative and slips it through the front door of the crate. Mom lets out terrified growls and hisses. Her claws scrape the plastic floor of the carrier, and one of the kits lets out a sound. It's thin and reedy, the sound of an animal that has never once had reason to feel safe.

She slides the needle into the skunk's thigh and jumps back as Mom sprays the inside of the carrier.

Fuck! That stink is going to stick.

She wraps herself around her babies again, and within a minute, her body goes slack, her breathing evening out.

"Okay." Luna lifts her out and lays her on the exam table as Ethan secures the cover on the crate again to contain the babies, who are crying for their mom.

Under the lights, the damage is worse. The foot sores are raw and weeping, caused when an animal stands on hardware cloth day after day with nowhere soft to rest. Her nipples are enlarged and cracked from nursing on an empty tank.

"She's been starving herself to feed them." Luna's fingers move along the skunk's ribcage. "Maren, get me a fluid setup. And pull the surgical tray. I have to ligate the scent glands before I can do a full workup."

Ligation is the temporary tying off of the ducts that connect the scent glands to the outside world, blocking the spray without removing the glands themselves. It's delicate work. Tie too tight and you damage the tissue. Too loose and you get a face full of thioacetate at close range, which is the chemical equivalent of pepper spray mixed with rotten eggs.

Everyone has smelled skunk spray at a distance, that roadkill perfume that drifts through your car windows on a summer highway. Up close, at full concentration, it's a different animal. It burns eyes, noses, and throats. It saturates fabric and skin and doesn't wash out for days.

Luna and Ethan work in tandem for an hour, while I assist, holding and passing instruments and keeping the kits warm under a heat lamp. She ligates first the mother's, then the kit's glands, her fingers moving with the steadiness and care of a woman who doesn't acknowledge the possibility of error. The smallest baby has a clouded left eye, likely from infection, and Luna flushes it and starts antibiotics before moving to the next.

By the time she finishes giving each one a bath, it's almost noon, and the treatment room smells like antiseptic and fear and skunk musk.

I throw open all the windows and doors as Ethan takes the crate outside to wash. We strip off our hazmat gear and seal it in a garbage bag.

"Shit, that smell is gonna stay around a while."

Luna sighs. "Get the de-skunking enzymes. We need to scrub everything down."

"How long are you going to keep them ligated?"

"Until they're stabilized and we can get an outdoor enclosure set up for them."

Luna stands at the table and looks at the four skunks, now bundled in a warming incubator, the mother on her side with the kits pressed against her belly, an IV line running, and monitors beeping their patient, repetitive count.

"He kept them on wire," Luna says through clenched teeth. "On wire, Maren."

"I know."

She braces both hands on the edge of the table. Her shoulders draw up toward her ears and hold there, the tendons in her forearms standing taut. Then she breathes one long exhale. Her shoulders drop, and her jaw unclenches. She turns to me, and she's Luna again.

"I think we should set up the outdoor enclosure on the east side. Behind the storage shed, far from the wolves. If they pick up skunk scent, it'll set off territorial responses, and I don't want to deal with that on top of everything else."

"I'll help."

"You don't have to."

"Bitch, please. If I don't, I'll have to fend off Ricky, and I'd much rather build a skunk enclosure."

We spend the early afternoon cleaning. The scent will linger for a few days regardless, but at least my eyes aren't watering anymore.

The enclosure is one of the smaller outdoor habitats, with chain-link walls, a privacy screen, brush piles inside for cover, and a shallow pan for water. Luna adds a denning box lined with cedar shavings and positions it under the overhang of the storage shed that abuts the enclosure.

"They'll want to be underground," she says, tucking straw into the den box. "Striped skunks are burrowers. This'll do until they're strong enough for release."

She stands, and I throw my arm over her shoulder.

"Where are we keeping them in the meantime?"

"Isolated in the recovery den."

"Good thing we don't have any other cases right now."

By the following Saturday, everyone is stable, and we install the skunk family in their enclosure. The mother orients herself, gathers her kits with her nose, and shuffles into the den box without looking back. The kits follow in a line, three small black and white bodies disappearing into the dark opening.

Luna stands at the enclosure fence and watches until there's nothing left to watch.

This is what she does. This is all she does.

I lean against the shed and study her profile. The afternoon light catches the angles of her face, the set of her mouth, and the way her eyes stay fixed on that den box opening as if the skunks might need her in the next thirty seconds and she intends to be ready. She's lost weight, not a lot, but enough that her jeans are looser and her collarbones are sharper than they were six months ago. She eats when I put food in front of her and forgets when I don't.

Her phone hasn't buzzed with a text that isn't mine in weeks. The last time she went to Nancy's for dinner was with me, two months ago, and she spent the entire meal checking her watch because a great horned owl was in critical recovery and she'd left Ethan monitoring him alone.

She lives here, and by that I don't mean she has a house on the property, though she does. But she lives here like the sanctuary is her circulatory system, and without it she'd flatline. Every animal that comes through those doors gets a piece of her, and she never takes any of it back. The wolves, the horses, the foxes, the raptors, the mountain lions, Ricky, and now these skunks. She pours and pours, and the cup never refills because there's no one pouring into her.

I want to say, "Luna, you need a life that isn't this. A person, a man, a woman, any warm body that talks back and makes you come so hard you forget about the owl for five minutes. You need to be selfish for one single hour. Let someone take care of you the way you take care of every broken thing that crosses your path."

But I don't. Because I've said it before, in different words, and she looks at me with those hazel eyes and says, "I'm fine, Mar," and means it. She doesn't see the gap. She doesn't register the absence. The sanctuary fills every space inside her, and she can't tell the difference between full and overflowing and running on fumes.

One day the absence is going to catch up with her. One day a person or a need or a want is going to walk through those doors, and she won't have the antibodies for it because she's never let herself be exposed.

I don't say any of that either. I bump her shoulder with mine and file my worry in the place where I keep all the worries about Luna that she'll never let me fix.

Chapter Thirteen

Damien

The average male human body holds between ten and twelve pints of blood, and Dale Nash is bleeding out fast.

He lies on the cold stainless-steel table in the center of the room, torso, legs, and ankles strapped down by thick leather belts. His arms are pinned so tight over his head that every shallow breath is a struggle. There isn't a position that doesn't hurt. I made sure of that.

This is my first kill in my new kill room. Jeremiah's former kill room. The master bedroom and office renovations are done upstairs, but I've given Jack and Genevieve instructions to step back for the moment. The permitting has turned into a nightmare. I think the county would prefer I raze the place rather than renovate it. We managed to get the mechanical systems' upgrades, except the plumbing, through before the building inspector started dragging his feet. But the temporary stay in work gives me an opportunity to settle into my space. Recalibrate and focus on more important things than pretty aesthetics.

Like the waste of a human life on my table. I roll my sleeves up to the elbow and step closer.

"Let's talk about your crimes, Dale."

His eyes fly open, pupils contracting to pinpoints, as they scan the silver titanium wolf mask that covers my face from the crown of my head to just above my upper lip. I always wear my mask when I punish them. Not because I need to hide my identity. My victims never leave alive. I wear it because it reveals my true nature. The second the cool metal touches my face, I am the wolf. The predator. The punisher of monsters.

Fresh sweat breaks out across Nash's forehead. He didn't expect me to know about his crimes. They never do. The duct tape turns his protest into a series of choking consonants as I reach for a folder at the edge of the workbench and flip it open. Photographs spill across the stained wood. Each one a testament to the kind of man strapped to my table.

"Thirty-seven elk. That's the number we confirmed."

I hold up the first photograph, angling it toward the light so Nash can see. A magnificent bull elk, its antlers sawed off at the base, the carcass left to bloat in a mountain meadow.

"You and your buddies ran a poaching operation out of Cheyenne for three years. Spotlighting herds at night. Shooting the bulls for their velvet antlers. Leaving the cows and calves to starve without the herd structure that keeps them alive through winter."

Nash's eyes dart between the photograph and my mask. His nostrils flare with each ragged breath.

I drop the photo and reach for another. A cow elk, ribs jutting through her hide, frozen stiff in a snow-choked ravine. A calf pressed against her flank, dead for weeks before anyone found them.

"Chinese black market pays what, eight hundred a pound for velvet antler?" I let the number hang in the air. "You butchered thirty-seven animals for grinding powder that rich men in Shanghai mix into their tea to get their dicks hard."

The folder contains more. Photographs of the salt licks laced with sedatives Nash used to bait the herds into open clearings. GPS coordinates of kill sites scattered across three counties and two states. Financial records tracing payments through a shell company in Laramie to a broker in San Francisco, who I will deal with soon enough. Cade spent eleven months building this file while Wyoming Game and Fish chased their own tails. The state issued Nash a fine. Twelve hundred dollars and a suspended hunting license.

I set the pictures down and pick up a pair of needle-nose pliers from the workbench. Nash's screams intensify behind the tape. I turn the pliers in the light, opening and closing the jaws with a soft metallic click. "You know how they harvest velvet from farmed elk? They restrain the animal in a crush chute. No anesthesia. Then they saw through the antlers while blood pours down the animal's face, and it thrashes so hard it breaks its own legs trying to escape."

I move to the table. Nash writhes, his heels drumming against the metal surface.

"But you didn't even bother with the chute, did you, Dale? You dropped them where they stood. One shot to the spine. Paralyzed but conscious while you went to work with your hacksaw." I lean close enough to watch my reflection swim in the wet terror of his eyes. "How long do you think they stayed aware? Five minutes? Ten?"

The pliers find the edge of the first cut on his chest. I grip a thin flap of skin between the serrated jaws and pull. The flesh stretches, separating from the muscle beneath with a wet, tearing sound.

Nash's back arches off the table. Every vein in his neck stands out. His scream vibrates through the duct tape. The sound feeds the hollow space inside me, filling it with a warmth no whiskey can match.

I step back. Blood sheets down his chest in a dark curtain, pooling in the hollow of his groin.

"That was one square inch, Dale. The average bull elk has roughly fifty square feet of hide." I wipe the pliers on my pants. "I'm no mathematician, but we've got a long way to go."

His body shakes in continuous tremors now, shock creeping in at the edges, trying to steal my canvas before I finish my work. I check the pulse in his throat. It's rapid but strong. Good. Nash is a big man. He'll last.

From the workbench, I retrieve a small glass vial and a syringe. Epinephrine. The body's own chemical against unconsciousness. I slide it into the muscle of Nash's thigh. His pupils blow wide, his heart rate surging under my fingertips. No drifting off or merciful darkness for him. He'll stay present for every second of this.

"There we go."

I return to the workbench and select a ball-peen hammer, and a fresh wave of panic floods Nash's face. The rain intensifies outside, drumming against the boarded window in sheets. Somewhere above us, a shutter bangs against the mansion's facade in irregular wind-driven blows.

I bring the hammer down on his left shin. The sound it makes is not what most people expect. It isn't a crack, but the wet, dense sound of tissue giving way before bone does. Nash's body arches off the table and comes back down, and the table moves with him, the legs scraping three inches across the concrete.

His eyes roll back, the pain and pure, primal terror overloading every circuit in his brain, but unconsciousness eludes him. The epinephrine won't let him escape. His body is a cage now, same as those elk, and his mind is the animal trapped inside.

The storm swallows his screams. The basement holds them in its stone belly like a secret it will never tell. Above us, Athena sleeps by the fire while the wolf beneath the mask restores the balance men like Nash destroy.

I move to his right leg. The elk don't get to rest between antlers. Neither does he.

His voice gives out before I'm done with the second leg, and his body has stopped pulling at the restraints, conserving energy, and hoarding its diminishing resources for survival. I set the hammer down and pick up the pliers again. I pause to check his vitals. His pulse is thready, and his blood pressure is dropping but not to a critical level yet.

The phone in my back pocket vibrates. I ignore it. Cade can wait.

It vibrates again. And again.

I set the pliers on the workbench and pull it out with a sigh. The screen shows three messages, each more urgent than the last.

Cade

Perimeter alert. West boundary.

> Motion sensors tripped. Large animal, maybe a vehicle. Can't confirm because of the weather.

> Satellite shows that sanctuary neighbor of yours. Her truck pulled into the turnout to the west of your drive.

My pulse spikes, and the man bleeding out on my table isn't the reason. The veterinarian next door. I've never seen her since I bought the place.

I look at Nash. His head lolls to one side, consciousness flickering behind half-closed lids. The epinephrine is wearing off.

The phone buzzes once more.

Cade

> She got out with a flashlight. Heading into the tree line.

> Should I grab the chopper and come up?

My jaw tightens beneath the mask. A woman with a flashlight is wandering the woods near my property line in the middle of the night in a storm while I have a man filleted open in my basement.

I pick up the syringe and slide it into Nash's thigh.

"Don't go anywhere, Dale."

His eyes snap open, wild and uncomprehending, as the chemical jolt rips him back to full awareness.

I wipe my hands with a towel before taking the stairs two at a time, stripping the mask as I go. Athena raises her head as I pass the office doorway, her ears pricked forward, reading the shift in my body language.

"Stay."

The front door groans as I ease it open. Rain drives cold and hard against my face as I step onto the porch and scan the treeline to the west.

A pinprick of light bobs through the trees. Moving away from my property line, stopping and starting again.

What the fuck is she doing out there?

She's tracking an animal. The realization hits with a certainty I can't explain. The way the light pauses, dips low, and then sweeps in an arc. She's following a trail.

My hands grip the porch railing. Splinters bite into my palms. Below me, in the basement, Nash bleeds. Above me, lightning fractures the sky, and in its flash, I catch the silhouette of a woman crouched in the center of the trees, one hand extended toward the darkness between the trunks.

The tightening behind my ribs returns, stronger this time. I pull out my phone and type a response to Cade.

Me

Stand down. I'll handle it.

The rain runs down my face and drips from my jaw as she stands, and her light disappears deeper into the forest. Every few steps the beam dips to the ground, lifts, and then drops again. She's still looking for whatever pulled her out here. The rain comes down harder, but she doesn't stop.

I should go back inside and finish what I started.

Instead, I step into the storm.

———— ◆◇◆ ————

The ground between the porch and the tree line is a minefield of exposed roots and rain-slicked grass. I move through it without breaking stride. The rain hammers my shoulders, saturating my blood-soaked clothes in seconds, turning the fabric into a second skin that clings to every muscle.

Fifty yards in, the ground slopes toward the creek, marking my property's boundary. High and swollen with rain, the water roars over the rocks. Lightning flashes again. Her silhouette, hidden under a lumpy rain slicker, crouches next to a fallen oak. Her infamous wolf stands at her left side, ears pinned forward, tail dropped, every muscle coiled under his wet coat. I pull back behind a pine and hold my breath.

Rain hammers the canopy above and fills every gap in the air. Through it, I can make out her voice, low and cautious, but the words dissolve in the din before they reach me. The clouds shift and moonlight comes down in a thin column through the trees. Her wolf is motionless beside her. He's locked onto whatever she's talking to in the brush in front of her.

A sound rips out of the dark tangle, half hiss, half growl, the sound of an animal with nowhere left to go. It rises, cracks, and then drops into a wet snarl that vibrates through the storm, warning everything within range that it still has teeth.

The wolf drops his head and growls back. One word from her and he goes quiet, but his eyes stay fixed on the root ball of the fallen tree, where two pale eyes burn low in the shadows, unblinking, caught in the beam of her headlamp.

She reaches a pole forward, inch by inch.

The clouds shift again, and I crouch, pressing my spine against the tree trunk, and wait. She keeps talking, her tone low, but the storm swallows most of her voice. What reaches me is a patient, level murmur threaded through the noise of the downpour, the sound of someone prepared to wait as long as it takes.

Another flash of lightning and I see her silhouette lean in, drawing an animal out with both hands. A young mountain lion, maybe, small and wrung out, its fur wet and matted. It hangs unconscious in her arms.

She turns, and her headlamp sweeps the tree line, the beam dragging through the rain and crossing the pine above my head. She pulls the cat higher against her chest and starts walking, still too far away and hidden in shadow for me to see clearly. The wolf walks close at her side, sniffing the dirt. Her path is straight, and she doesn't look back, heading through the trees toward the road. Toward her truck.

The wolf's head comes up.

His hackles lift along his spine, and he turns his nose into the rain, toward me, his nostrils flaring. The growl starts deep in his chest, quiet at first, then gaining volume. My pulse thrums hard in my throat. He has my scent. There's no question about it.

Neither of us moves.

Then the growl drops off, and his hackles smooth out. He swings his nose back toward the brush and exhales.

Her voice carries through the storm again as she calls back to him. The words drift to me faint and shapeless at the edges, but I can just make them out this time.

"What were you growling at, baby?"

I look at the animal, the height of him, the breadth of his chest, and the way he takes up space in the dark, and the corner of my mouth lifts.

She calls that thing baby?

The wolf returns to her side. The light swings off, resuming its retreat, shrinking to a pale firefly beyond the trunks until it finally dies.

The rain beats down on my head. I hold my position against the trunk and watch the dark where her light used to be. Several minutes pass. The darkness between the trees stays solid and unbroken, and the forest holds its breath with me.

Then, from the road, an engine turns over. The starter coughs and catches, and her truck rumbles to life. Headlights push through the trees, turning the rain gold for one brief second before they swing west, carrying her and her stray passenger back toward her sanctuary.

I stay crouched for another minute, listening. Nothing moves. She was alone, with her wolf, chasing an injured animal along a property line that borders a house where a man is being skinned alive. The recklessness tightens my hands into fists against the rock.

Water cascades off my shoulders and down my back. The return climb from the creek is slower, uphill, until the mansion emerges from the trees. Its empty windows watch me cross the overgrown lawn.

On the porch, I pause and strip the soaked shirt over my head, wringing it out. My phone vibrates.

I drape the shirt over the railing and push open the front door. Athena meets me in the hallway. Her nose presses into my palm, and I stroke her head.

"Good girl."

The basement door waits at the end of the hall. Behind it is Dale Nash and his thirty-seven elk and the debt his body owes the dead.

I descend the stairs, and the door swings shut behind me. The storm, the woman, the wolf, and that mysterious wild cat become a memory the house seals in its bones alongside forty years of secrets.

My mask waits on the bottom step. I pick it up, the titanium cold against my fingers, and slip it on.

The man who stood in the rain watching a stranger's headlamp vanish into the dark ceases to exist.

And the wolf returns to his work.

Chapter Fourteen

Maren

The skunks settle in.

Over the next several weeks they become the sanctuary's quietest residents and its most stubborn. Luna removes the ligations once the kits are strong enough to handle the stress of the procedure reversal, and within days of being in their new den enclosure, the mother demonstrates why skunks have survived for millions of years by being the most passive-aggressive creatures on the planet.

She doesn't spray. She doesn't need to. She lifts her tail, assumes the position, and every animal within a fifty-yard radius decides it has somewhere else to be. The wolves, three enclosures and two hundred yards away, pace and whine for an hour after the first time she does it, picking up the faintest trace on the wind.

The kits grow. The cloudy-eyed one, who Luna names Pepper because she refuses to let me name any more animals after my suggestion of Pepe Le Pew was rejected on the grounds of being insensitive to skunks, clears up on antibiotics and starts using that eye to track Luna's movements like a very small, very committed private investigator. The other two are Clove and Basil, and of course the mom is Oregano because Luna has a spice theme going, and I've made my peace with it.

I'm in the clinic sterilizing instruments with Ricky in his wrap because it's a clingy day. He's rooting around, trying to get his hands and face down the front of my shirt when Jenny, our newest intern, comes in.

"Ah, Maren. Luna needs you."

We find her on her hands and knees inside the enclosure. She has her cheek pressed to the dirt, a flashlight aimed under the two-inch gap between the storage shed's foundation and the ground.

"They tunneled under the shed."

"Of course they did."

Ricky wriggles in the wrap, eager to get out, so I set him on the grass. He makes a beeline for Luna and tries to wedge his head into the hole alongside hers.

"The mother excavated a proper den. Under my storage shed. With three exits that I can see."

"Industrious."

Luna grabs Ricky around the belly and hauls him back without looking. He pivots in her grip and makes a grab for her chest like that was his plan all along.

"This isn't funny, Maren. I have four unreleasable skunks with active scent glands living under a building that houses three thousand dollars' worth of veterinary supplies and feed."

"So she's squatting. Moved into the basement without signing a lease. Very Gen Z of her."

Luna sits back on her heels, lifting Ricky against her chest. He goes straight for her boobs with both hands, but she's too distracted to notice. Dirt streaks her forehead and her left cheek. A piece of straw clings to her blonde hair above her ear. She looks up at me with the expression of a woman who loves animals with her whole being and is currently reconsidering every choice that led her to this exact spot on the ground.

"I need to extract them."

"From a den that a skunk built. Under a building with three exits." I crouch beside her. "Luna, that's not extraction. That's war."

"It's humane removal."

"Call it what you want. You're going to war with a skunk."

⸺ ◦ ⸺

It takes six days.

Six days of Luna on her belly in the dirt with a flashlight and a have-a-heart trap baited with sardines.

Six days of the mother skunk relocating her kits through whichever exit Luna isn't watching.

Six days of me standing upwind, often with Ricky strapped to my chest, his little hand grabbing for my boobs like he's paid for the privilege, as I hand Luna supplies and offer commentary she does not appreciate but needs anyway.

Day one: Luna blocks two exits with hardware cloth. The mother digs a fourth.

Day two: Luna blocks the fourth exit. The mother digs a fifth, this one angled under the concrete pad at the back of the shed, which is impressive for an animal with a brain the size of a walnut.

"She's smarter than my last three boyfriends combined," I tell Luna, who's lying face-down in gravel with her arm shoved under the shed up to her shoulder.

"Your last three boyfriends set a low bar."

"Excuse me. JT is a good guy."

"Yes. But he once microwaved a fork."

"He was tired."

Day three: the sardine trap catches Basil. Luna transfers him to a secure carrier and resets the trap. That night, the mother moves Pepper and Clove to a secondary chamber she's excavated deeper under the foundation, beyond Luna's reach and further from the trap.

Day four: Luna brings in a borescope camera, threading the flexible cable through the tunnel entrance. On the tiny screen, the mother skunk stares straight into the lens with a look that transcends species. Pure, uncut contempt.

"She hates you," I say.

"She doesn't hate me. She's protecting her family."

"She hates you, and she's protecting her family. Both things can be true. I hate JT when he leaves the toilet seat up, but I still protect him from my grandmother."

Day five: Luna rethinks the approach. Instead of blocking exits, she opens all of them and places sardine traps at each one, creating what she calls a voluntary extraction matrix and what I call an all-you-can-eat buffet for a squatter.

Day six: By morning, Pepper is in trap two and Clove is in trap four. The mother sits at the main entrance of her den, tail raised, watching Luna collect the carriers with the energy of a woman who will burn this entire shed to the ground before she surrenders.

I've parked myself cross-legged in the grass behind her, Ricky loose in my lap. He rolls backward onto the ground, then turns onto his belly. He plants both hands in the clover and pulls, coming up with a fistful, before moving six inches and doing it again.

Luna places the three kits in carriers outside the main tunnel entrance. They chitter. They cry. They make the sounds that baby skunks make when they want their mom, which turns out to be a noise calibrated by evolution to be impossible to ignore.

And Ricky, it seems, is not immune.

He locks onto the carriers.

"Ricky, don't you—"

I reach for him, but he's already moving, a low, determined scramble through the grass, faster than his little legs have any right to go. Luna lunges from the left. I lunge from the right. He goes straight through the gap between our hands and launches himself toward the carriers as the mother emerges.

She doesn't hesitate. Her tail goes up, and the spray hits Ricky square in the chest, the overspray hitting me.

"Oh no." Luna presses both hands over her nose and mouth.

For one long second I stand there while my eyes and throat catch fire. Ricky recoils and sits down hard, gagging and blinking, as I drop to my knees and vomit into the grass.

The good news is my chest took the hit, not my face. My girls have never earned their keep more in my thirty-two years on this earth. The bad news is my shirt is saturated, and tears are running down my face, and my lungs feel like they're about to explode.

Ricky is on the grass, looking up at me with watery eyes of his own, and sneezes.

"God, Mar. Are you alright?"

"You little shit." The cough that follows scrapes all the way up from my chest.

I get my feet under me and get both hands under Ricky's arms, holding him away from my body, but it's a lost cause. The smell is all over me. I carry him to the enclosure at arm's length while he dangles, unbothered, legs swinging. Raccoons are less sensitive to skunk spray than other animals and humans, but he's still pawing at his face and drooling, so it wasn't a free pass either.

I latch the door behind him. He sits in the cedar shavings and looks at me through the wire like he doesn't understand what he did. Drool collects at the corner of his mouth and drops. He sneezes into the shavings and looks back up at me.

The kits are still crying. A coughing fit doubles me over, and when I straighten, Luna is positioned at the corner of the shed, the trap in her hands, watching the mother move from carrier to carrier, nose pressed to each door, checking each kit, her body strung tight.

Then she turns and walks into the trap. Luna closes the door and sits in the grass and doesn't move for a long time. I sit down next to her. From the enclosure beside us, Ricky sneezes twice in quick succession and then goes quiet.

She looks at me. "You reek."

"No shit."

She shuffles away, her nose tucked into her collar. I follow her. She holds up a hand.

"You can't sit next to me right now."

My eyes burn, the shed swimming in front of me. I reach up to rub them and catch myself. My shirt is saturated, and my hands have been all over Ricky, and there is nothing I can do about any of it. Fuck!

I grab the hem and tear my shirt over my head and pitch it into the grass.

Luna glances toward the main building. "You remember Tate's here today, right?"

"I don't give a fuck. I can't breathe. At least it's a good bra day." I readjust and take a breath that does nothing for the burning in my chest. "I'm going to strangle that little shit. I shouldn't have taken him out of the wrap. That's on me. But I'm still going to strangle him."

"We need to get you and Ricky into a peroxide wash before the oils set in." Luna lifts her hand and makes a slow circle in the air between us, a gesture that covers the bra, the hair, and the full scope of the disaster. "Good thing JT's out of town."

"Right? He'd never have sex with me again." I tip my head back and look at the sky for a moment. "I'm sleeping in your bed tonight."

"You're gonna sleep in the barn and be grateful I'm not making you sleep outside."

"I'm climbing into your bed and pressing my entire skunky body against you. And there's nothing you can do about it."

She shifts a little further away.

"I'll build you a very comfortable hay situation next to Patches. With a good blanket." Her lips quirk. "He won't mind."

I know she's not serious, but I still want to rub my contaminated body all over her like a cat, just to watch the horror on her face when I do it.

She turns her head toward the carriers, and her shoulders drop. The tease goes out of her face, and she looks at the kits and the mother in the trap and lets out a slow breath. She's covered in six days' worth of dirt and the exhaustion that comes from outsmarting a creature that wasn't trying to be outsmarted but was simply trying to keep her children safe.

I pull a water bottle from my pocket and hold it across the distance between us.

"You need that more than I do."

I shake my hand at her. "I've got another one."

She reaches for it without getting close enough to touch me. I take a swig from my own and rinse the vomit taste out of my mouth.

"I'm releasing them."

"They're not ready."

"They're ready. The kits are almost weaned. The mother's foot sores are healed. The eye is clear." She turns the water bottle in her hands. "She doesn't want to be here, Mar. She wants to be wild, and she wants her babies wild, and every day I keep her in a cage, even a nice cage, even a cage with cedar shavings and a shallow water pan..." She sighs. "I'm the guy with the chicken wire in Masonville."

"You are nothing like that guy."

"I'm a different version. A kinder version. But I'm still the one deciding where she lives."

This is the thing about Luna that breaks my heart. She holds herself to a standard that would crush a normal person. Every decision gets weighed on a scale, and the thumb is always on the side that says you could have done more.

The breeze picks up. It hits me first, then Luna beside me. We both gag at the same moment, and it triggers another violent coughing fit.

Grass rustles to our right. Ricky emerges from the ground like he's done it a hundred times, picking his way out of one of the tunnel openings, ears up, rubbing his eyes with his fingers.

We both stare at him. He's a blur from where I'm sitting.

"He found one of the tunnels." Luna sounds impressed.

He stumbles through the grass, probably because his vision is just as hazy as mine, but he gives the carriers a wide berth.

"Oh, so now you know better."

He reaches me and climbs my shin, pulls himself into my lap, and drops there like he owns it. He tips his drooling, snotty, drippy-eyed little face up at me, then presses his cheek against my left breast and drags it back and forth.

"He's marking you," Luna says. "It's a bonding behavior."

"Luna, I swear to God."

She turns away, lifting the water bottle to her lips, a chuckle escaping as she swallows.

Ricky sneezes, then pats my boob twice and closes his eyes.

⸙

Luna waits one more week before releasing them. We drive the skunk family to a site she selected on BLM land north of the sanctuary with dense scrub, creek access, and existing burrow systems from ground squirrels that will give the mother a head start on den construction.

Luna opens the carrier in the tall grass and steps back.

The mother comes out first, nose up, tail down. Then she moves through the tall stems with confidence, like an animal whose wildness returns between one step and the next.

The three kits follow in their line, Pepper last, with the healed eye bright and open. They disappear into the scrub and don't look back.

Luna watches the spot where they vanished. The wind moves her hair across her face, and she doesn't push it away. Her hands hang at her sides, open, empty, the way they always are after a release. She gives and gives, and then she stands in a field and watches the thing she gave to walk away, and she calls it enough, calls it the job, and calls it her calling.

But I'm close enough to catch the faint tremor in her jaw. The quick blinks. The breath that hitches once before she masters it.

She needs a person who stays and arms that close around her after the field is empty and the animal is gone and the quiet rushes in. I can only fill so many of the spaces and the biggest ones, the ones that ache at three in the morning when the sanctuary is dark and Shadow is asleep and the bed is wide and cold. Those aren't mine to fill.

She doesn't see it. She'll never see it until it's standing in front of her, and even then she'll probably try to rehabilitate it and release it back into the wild.

We drive back in silence. A week ago I smelled like the inside of a skunk, courtesy of one small raccoon with no sense of consequences. Ricky smelled fresh and clean by the next morning, thanks to the Skunk Off Luna doused him in that night, which was unfair because I was doused in it too, but my hair held onto the smell for three days before it was gone. Now we're both fine, but my favorite bra was ruined, and the little menace will never apologize.

But today's a good day. The kind of day that reminds me why I'm here, why I drive up this mountain six days a week and work for a salary that wouldn't cover rent in Denver.

And why I let a raccoon molest me and a skunk teach me humility.

◆

The next morning, I feed Ricky his breakfast, a mix of scrambled eggs, banana, and his favorite blueberries. Luna is across the room, logging intake notes on her laptop, a pen tucked behind her ear because she still takes handwritten notes on everything before she duplicates all her work on the computer.

Ricky finishes his banana slices and blueberries. He ignores the scrambled eggs, which is unusual, and sits beside his dish, looking up at me with his blueberry-stained hands folded in his lap and his masked face pointed at mine, waiting for me to catch up.

"What?"

He chitters. That sound he makes when he's working up to a decision.

"Ricky, I swear on Estella's rosary, if you try anything—"

He launches from the table, both paws landing on my boobs, his back feet scrambling up my stomach, and before I can get my hands on him, he shoves his entire face down my shirt, between my breasts, and vibrates.

His whole body is buzzing, his nose pressed into my cleavage, his tiny mouth making a sound I can only describe as brrrrrrrrr against the skin above my bra, his head whipping side to side with the commitment of an animal who has found his purpose on this earth and will not be deterred.

My vibrator has a lower setting than this.

I freeze. My hands hover on either side of him, my fingers spread, my brain short-circuiting.

Luna makes a choking sound, and I turn my head. Ricky's still vibrating between my breasts, his small paws gripping the fabric of my shirt over each one. Luna's mouth is open, and her eyes are wide as I meet them.

"Is he motorboating me?"

The silence holds for one second.

Then Luna loses it.

She folds forward over the laptop, forehead hitting the keyboard, and the sound that comes out of her is airless, the kind of laugh that lives in the basement of your body and only comes up when the universe delivers a moment so absurd that your nervous system gives up trying to process it through normal channels.

Ricky pulls his face out of my cleavage. He sits back on my stomach, both paws still gripping my shirt, and looks up at me. His whiskers are bent sideways. A strand of my hair is stuck to his nose.

"This is assault. This is sexual harassment in the workplace. I want to speak to HR."

"I'm HR," Luna wheezes from the keyboard.

"Then you're complicit. You raised this pervert."

"So did you."

Ricky chitters at me, the rolling, self-satisfied sound he makes when he's unrepentant, which is always. Then he turns, climbs down my front, and scurries back to his dish to eat the scrambled eggs he ignored five minutes ago like nothing happened. Like he didn't cross a line that no raccoon rehabilitation manual has ever needed to address because no one in the history of wildlife medicine anticipated this specific scenario.

Luna lifts her head from her laptop. Her face is red, her eyes are watering, and the pen behind her ear has fallen into her collar.

"I have to put this in his behavioral log."

"What are you going to write? 'Patient demonstrates persistent mammary fixation with new motorboating component'?"

She snorts. "I'm going to write that he exhibited repetitive contact-seeking behavior with vibratory vocalization directed at the handler's chest area."

"Handler's chest area. That's what we're calling my tits now. I can't believe your rescue raccoon gave me better action than JT did before he left last week."

Luna wipes her eyes with the back of her hand as Ricky eats his eggs with both paws, an animal with nothing on his conscience. He is, by every measurable standard, a healthy, thriving, well-adjusted juvenile raccoon with a perversion that defies scientific explanation.

I look down at my chest. Two small dark blue, almost purple, paw prints sit centered on each boob like a signature.

I have paw prints on my boobs.

"I'm getting a T-shirt made."

Luna looks up at me, confused. "What's it going to say?"

"Ricky was here."

Chapter Fifteen

Luna

Ricky has developed a full-on boob fetish, and none of us have been left unscathed.

Six months ago, I unwrapped a half-dead, two-week-old raccoon from a towel and promised I'd do everything to save him. The universe, in its infinite wisdom, has rewarded my compassion by gifting me a furry little pervert, as Maren likes to call him, who treats every woman's chest like his personal pillow fort.

The coffee warms my palms through the mug as I watch him and Zorro navigate their morning routines. The chaos of their introduction aside, Zorro took Ricky under his wing almost right away. Now they live together in relative harmony. Most of the time. Sometimes feeding times get a little tricky, but we usually take Ricky out of the cage. Zorro doesn't like to come out. He prefers to stay in his space. But Ricky wants out all the time because while the enclosure has food, water, and Zorro, there's not a single boob in there.

Today, our resident senior raccoon perches on the highest platform, grooming his belly. Ricky sits on the one below him, investigating a puzzle feeder I loaded with grapes and apple slices at six this morning, working one paw into the feeder's rotating chamber.

He's filled out. The xylophone of ribs I traced those first terrible nights is buried under a healthy layer of fat and muscle. His coat gleams. His eyes are bright, black, and always scheming.

"You're staring at him again."

Maren appears beside me with her own coffee, her scrub shirt already sporting a mysterious stain near the hem. She leans against my side and peers into the enclosure.

"I'm doing my morning assessment."

"You're doing your morning heart-eyes. There's a difference."

I take a sip of coffee and don't argue, because somewhere between the subcutaneous fluids and the sleepless nights and the first time Ricky pressed his little face against the skin above my collar, I crossed a line. The clinical detachment I'm supposed to maintain, the professional distance I depend on, that part that makes release decisions possible, evaporated like morning fog over the mountains.

He's not going anywhere. I've run the calculations a dozen times, weighed the variables, and consulted the rehabilitation criteria. A raccoon with his level of human imprinting and his absolute refusal to fear people, releasing him would be a death sentence dressed up as freedom.

That's the justification, anyway. The real reason sits deeper in my chest, in a place that's the reason why we have twenty-seven permanent residents at the sanctuary.

In the enclosure, Ricky cracks the puzzle feeder and stuffs three grapes into his mouth at once. Zorro glances down from his platform, takes in the situation, and looks away. He didn't choose this arrangement but he's accepted it. When Ricky first moved in, I braced for territorial aggression, resource guarding, and the usual friction. Instead, Zorro sniffed Ricky once, stole a blueberry from his food dish, and went to sleep. They've been fine ever since.

I turn and head to my office. Maren follows. She pauses at the door, one hand on the frame.

"Hey, I've been meaning to ask you. Have you met your new neighbor yet?"

"No. Why?"

"I followed a big delivery truck up this morning. It turned into his driveway."

"There's been trucks in and out of there for the past couple of weeks."

"Well, I think you should go over and introduce yourself. Eleanor said he's hot as fuck. Nancy agreed."

"I don't think Eleanor or Nancy talk like that."

"They do when describing your new neighbor. I think you should take him a casserole and welcome him to the neighborhood. And wear your green tank top. It shows off your assets."

"I don't have time to bake casseroles."

"You don't bake a casserole. You assemble one. Actually, I guess you do bake it, but that's not the point. It's the sluttiest dish in existence. It's basically foreplay. Soft, warm, just everything sliding into everything else."

"Please stop sexualizing casseroles."

"Whatever, I've got to check on Winston."

Winston is an opossum who came in a few days ago with an infected eye. I had to remove it. The socket is healing, but Winston's disposition is not.

"How's his eye this morning?"

"It looked okay last night when I checked it," Maren says. "But I'm going to clean it now and put a fresh bandage on. I still can't believe you didn't name him One-eyed Willie. It's such a great name."

"It's not a name. It's a pirate and a penis joke."

"It's a cinematic reference, and those are the best kinds of jokes. Nevermind, I'm done with you."

She disappears down the corridor before I can respond.

⸻◆⸻

I settle into my desk chair and open my laptop, pulling up the new grant application I started yesterday, but my eyes drift toward the window. From this angle, the Morrison estate is on the other side of that dense thicket of trees.

Hot as fuck.

I roll my eyes at the empty room. Eleanor is seventy-eight years old, still dyes her hair jet black, and wears enormous rhinestone glasses. She runs the post office with the iron grip of a woman who has read everyone's mail for five decades. If she's commenting on a man's appearance, he's either a movie star or she's lost it.

But a subtle undercurrent of curiosity persists beneath my morning's task. Whoever this man is, he's my second closest neighbor now, and proximity matters when you're running a facility full of animals that scream, howl, and chatter at all hours. I should go over. Bring him Maren's ridiculous casserole. Introduce myself and the reality of living next to a wildlife sanctuary before he calls the sheriff about the noise.

But not today. Today I have too damn much to do. I'm halfway through the application when the front door of the main building slams open hard enough to rattle the framed wildlife prints on the corridor wall.

"Luna!"

The voice cracks on my name, and I'm out of my chair and down the hallway before my coffee cup stops rocking on the desk.

Old Man Henderson is in the lobby, chest heaving, his face the color of wet cement. His battered baseball cap is gone, and sweat plasters thin white hair to his forehead. His shirt is off, bundled against his chest, and his undershirt is soaked through. He's cradling the bundle like a newborn, and his hands are shaking so bad the fabric trembles.

"I didn't see her. God help me, Luna, I didn't see her."

I cross the lobby in four steps and guide him toward the exam room. "Bring her in here. Tell me what happened."

"The weed whacker. She was under a thicket, tucked in the brush pile by the back fence. I didn't know. I didn't..." His voice breaks apart. A sound comes out of him that I've only ever associated with grief. A raw, wet noise with nowhere left to go.

I ease the shirt open on the exam table.

A fox squirrel, maybe a year old, lies curled on her side. Her dark eyes are wide, and her pupils are blown. Her breathing is rapid and shallow, her tiny chest pumping too fast. Blood soaks the lower half of the fabric, and the source is clear. Her tail is gone from about three inches past the base. What remains is a ragged stump, the vertebrae visible through torn muscle. But there's a red bandana tied tight around the severed end, a crude tourniquet that is the only reason this animal still has a pulse.

"Mr. Henderson, did you tie this?"

"I grabbed it off my neck. I didn't know what else to do. There was so much blood."

"You did the right thing. Go sit in the lobby. I need to work."

"Is she going to—"

I give him my most calming smile. I won't give him a promise I don't know yet if I can keep.

"It's okay. Let me work on her."

Maren appears in the doorway. Her gaze drops to the squirrel, then to the blood-soaked fabric, and then to me. She moves to the supply cabinet and starts pulling what I need before I ask for it.

"Tate," she calls, and he comes rushing in from the lobby. "Get Henderson a glass of water before he passes out." Her eyes soften. "We'll come find you."

Tate leads him back toward the lobby.

I snap on gloves. "I need the small mammal surgical kit and blood for a transfusion."

"Already ahead of you."

The squirrel's body temperature is critically low. I wrap a warm towel around her torso while I assess her condition. Her gums are pale but not white. She's dehydrated, shocky, but alive, and the bandana tourniquet kept her from bleeding out on the run over.

Maren gets the isoflurane running to put her under. I loosen the bandana, and fresh blood wells up. I clamp the bleeder, irrigate the wound, and start working. The tail vertebrae are shattered at the cut point, bone fragments embedded in the surrounding tissue. I debride the dead flesh and remove the fragments.

"Suture."

Maren places the needle in my palm. I tie off the vessel, then begin closing the stump. The skin is mangled, but there's enough viable tissue to create a flap. My hands are steady, the stitches small and precise, each one pulling the wound closed millimeter by millimeter.

The squirrel twitches under the light anesthesia. Her back leg kicks once.

"Feisty little thing," Maren murmurs.

"Feisty is good. It means she's a fighter."

I step back. The squirrel lies on the table, her breathing slower now, more even. The stump is closed and no longer bleeding. She'll have about three inches of tail left when this heals. Enough for balance. Maybe enough for the full rudder function a squirrel relies on in the canopy, but that's another release calculation I'll have to run later.

I set up a small recovery cage in the den and line it with fleece. I tuck a warming pad under one side, then transfer her from the operating table. She stirs as I settle her onto the pad, one dark eye cracking open. Her front paw swipes at my glove with surprising coordination for an animal still under the effects of anesthesia.

"Yeah, you're going to be fine, pretty girl."

I walk out to the lobby. Old Man Henderson is sitting in the chair by the front window, his elbows on his knees, his face buried in his hands. Maren sits beside him with one arm around his shoulders, her voice low as she talks to him. She's given him one of the sanctuary hoodies to wear, even though it's eighty degrees outside.

He looks up at the sound of my footsteps on the tile. He has an old man's face, the kind that doesn't hide much anymore, and right now his eyes are red-rimmed and still wet.

"She's going to be okay."

His whole body sags. He stands, crosses the lobby, and wraps his arms around me. He's thin and wiry and smells like cut grass and the sharp tang of sweat. I hug him back.

"That bandana you tied around her tail saved her life, Mr. Henderson. She would've bled out before you got here without it."

He pulls back and wipes his eyes with the heel of his hand. "I just did it. I didn't think."

"Your instincts were perfect."

He turns and hugs Maren. She pats his back and meets my eyes over his shoulder.

"I'm going to keep her for a week, maybe two. I want to monitor the wound site and make sure there's no infection. She lost a lot of blood, so she needs time to recover."

"Can I come see her?"

"Every day if you want."

He nods, his chin trembling. "I checked that brush pile last week. She wasn't there last week."

"Animals move around. It's not your fault."

"It is my fault. I should have looked again."

Maren squeezes his arm. "Henderson, if everyone who accidentally hurt a squirrel went to prison, the entire state of Colorado would be behind bars. You brought her here. You saved her. You're a rock star."

He manages a weak smile, and his eyes drift toward the corridor.

"She's gonna be here over twenty-four hours. She needs a name," Maren announces with a sly grin. "And it's my turn. Luna got to name Winston, and she wasted it on a boring one when I had a brilliant one lined up."

I'm about to argue with her again, but I know she's trying to lighten the moment. Henderson wipes his nose on his sleeve.

"She should be called Sassy."

Maren and I both look at him.

"She swiped at me when I picked her up. Tail half gone, bleeding everywhere, and she still took a swing. That's a sassy little girl. Too sassy to be kept down."

Maren tilts her head. For a second, I brace for a fight because she guards her naming rights like a dragon on a gold pile.

"Sassy." She tests it on her tongue. "Okay. I'll allow it. But only because it was your idea and because I respect a woman who fights back when life literally cuts off her best asset."

"Please, for the love of God, no tail innuendo."

"I would never. But now that you mention it…"

Henderson laughs, which I know was Maren's intention. It's watery and thin, but it's real. The color is returning to his face.

"I'll be back tomorrow morning. And I'm bringing her the good stuff from the garden. Butternut squash, and some of those sugar snap peas."

"She'll love the peas," I say. "Squirrels go crazy for sugar snaps."

He nods, adjusts the borrowed sweatshirt, and shuffles toward the door. He pauses with his hand on the knob.

"Thank you, Luna. You too, Maren. You're good girls."

Maren snorts. "That's the first time I've been called that in a long time. Tate?"

He comes through the swinging door.

"Grab the keys to Luna's truck and drive Mr. Henderson home, please."

Tate nods and heads into the back to get the keys.

"I can walk," Henderson insists.

"The hell you will, old man. You just ran here like a marathoner."

"Maren's right," I say. "Let Tate drive you home. I won't take no for an answer. Get some rest, and I can come over this weekend and help you finish up that weed whacking."

Tate returns and leads Henderson out. The door closes behind them, and Maren drops into the chair and exhales.

"Well. That was a hell of a way to start a Monday."

"It's Wednesday."

"Shit."

⚬

Maren pushes herself to her feet.

"Come on. Let's go clean up before the blood dries on everything."

I nod and follow her down the hall. The exam table looks like a crime scene. Henderson's shirt is still crumpled by the sink, rust-brown and stiff where the blood has already set. I gather it up and toss it into the biohazard bin while Maren runs the autoclave and wipes down the instrument trays.

We work in silence, the kind that only exists between two people who have done this a thousand times together. Maren scrubs the table while I restock the surgical kit. The mundane inventory of a life spent putting small broken bodies back together.

By the time the room is spotless and the instruments are cycling through sterilization, my shoulders are screaming and my stomach is eating itself. We drift toward the kitchen.

I pour myself a glass of water and lean against the counter as Maren opens the fridge and pulls out a bowl of raspberries. I pop a few into my mouth as we stand there in the quiet, both of us decompressing.

Tate comes ambling in, red-faced from the heat, lugging an enormous wicker basket overflowing with produce. Tomatoes, zucchini, yellow squash, green beans, a couple of fat cucumbers, and snap peas for Sassy. He sets it on the counter with a grunt.

"Henderson insisted. Said he's bringing more tomorrow."

The basket is ridiculous. There's enough here to feed the entire staff for a week. I pick up a tomato the size of a softball and turn it over in my hands. It's warm from the sun, the skin deep red, and it smells like dirt and summer.

"I could make garden vegetable soup with all of this. Roast the tomatoes and throw in the zucchini."

Maren looks at me like I've lost my mind. "It's the middle of freaking August. It's almost eighty degrees outside. You want to stand over a boiling pot and make soup."

"Soup is comforting."

"You know what else is comforting? Ice cream. A cold shower. Literally anything that doesn't involve simmering vegetables in a kitchen with no air conditioning."

"I have air conditioning in my house. And I like soup."

"And I like orgasms, but there's a time and a place, Lu. This is not the time for soup." She grabs a tomato from the basket and bites into it like an apple. "This is the time for cold things. Salad. Gazpacho. A margarita."

Tate opens his mouth to weigh in, but a high-pitched squeal rips through the building from the direction of the main treatment area.

Tate nearly trips over his feet. Maren drops the tomato on the counter. I'm through the kitchen door and down the corridor in seconds, my feet skidding on the tile as I round the corner.

Katie, our newest intern, is standing in the middle of the room with her arms pinned to her sides and Ricky attached to the front of her scrub top. His back paws are braced against her stomach. His front paws have disappeared into her neckline. His face is buried down her shirt, and his head is moving side to side with a motion that can only be described as vigorous.

Katie is making a noise somewhere between a scream and a laugh, her face scarlet, her hands fluttering at her sides like she's afraid to touch him.

"Get him off! Get him off. Oh my God, he's in my bra!"

I wrap both hands around Ricky's arms. I have to peel him off finger by finger while Katie whimpers and holds very still.

"I'm so sorry, Katie. I'm so sorry."

Ricky comes free with a soft ripping sound. A button from Katie's scrub top pings off the floor and rolls under the exam table. He chitters in protest, his arms still reaching toward her chest as I pull him against my hip.

"Are you okay? Did he scratch you?"

Katie pulls her neckline up and peers down the front of her shirt. "I don't think so. He was messing with the lock on the enclosure, so I opened the door to see what he was doing and... he jumped."

"I know. He does that. I should have warned you. I'm sorry. Take a break."

She nods, still flushed, and retreats toward the lobby with her hand pressed flat against her chest like she's guarding it.

I hold Ricky at arm's length and look him in the eye. He blinks at me, his whiskers twitch, and he has the audacity to lick his nose.

"You. My office. Now."

I carry him down the corridor, one arm clamped around his middle. He's purring. The little menace is actually purring. I push through my office door, closing it behind me, and drop onto the sofa with him in my lap.

"We need to talk."

He stares at me with those angelic, innocent black marble eyes. A con artist in fur.

"You can't keep doing this. You can't launch yourself at people's chests. You're going to get me sued, and then where will you live? A zoo? You want to live in a zoo?"

He reaches up and touches my cheek with one paw, a look of pure innocence on his face. His fingers are cool and soft.

"Don't try to charm me. I'm serious. No more boobs that aren't mine or Maren's. That's the rule. Two sets of boobs. That's your allotment."

He chitters and then lays his head against my chest. Right in the center, his ear pressed flat over my sternum. His body relaxes, all the manic energy draining out of him like air from a balloon. His eyes half-close, and his breathing slows, as his hand settles on my right breast.

I lean my head back against the cushion and let my hand rest on his back.

The door opens, and Maren slides in, chuckling.

"Katie's fine. She's in the lobby drinking Tate's emergency Dr. Pepper and calling her mom."

I whip my head up. "Calling her mom?"

"She needs to process. She said, and I quote, 'A raccoon just got to second base with me, and I don't know how to feel about it.'"

"This is a lawsuit waiting to happen."

Maren drops onto the other end of the sofa, kicks her shoes off, and stretches her legs out. She tips her head back and closes her eyes. Ricky lifts his face from my chest.

He scrambles off me and crosses the cushion between us, hauling himself up onto Maren's chest. She grunts at the impact but doesn't open her eyes. He circles once, twice, kneading her scrub top with his front paws, and then flattens himself against her like a furry pancake. His chin rests in the hollow of her throat.

"Great. My turn."

"He loves you."

"He loves my cup size. There's a difference." Maren strokes down his back, and he lets out a contented chitter. "He did the same thing to Annie on Friday when you were in town."

"What?"

"It was hilarious. She's standing there with a raccoon in her shirt, and I'm trying not to laugh because she's a very nice girl and she was very upset, Luna, and I should not have been laughing."

"But you were laughing."

"I was crying actual tears. Tate had to peel him off her because every time I got close, I started laughing again."

"Why didn't you tell me when I got back?"

"I forgot. The coyote came in and things went crazy."

I sigh. "That's the third female intern this month."

"Fourth. You're forgetting about the incident with Priya, which, credit to her, she handled like a champ. She stood frozen and said, 'He's on me.'"

"This is a liability nightmare."

"This is the best thing that's ever happened around here."

Maren's eyes are bright and feral. I glare at her.

"I'm serious. If one of these interns files a complaint, I'm going to get sued. We can't let any of the females handle him anymore. Only you and me."

"Because you and I have already accepted our roles as his favorite squeeze toys."

I press my fingers into my eyes. "Because you and I understand the situation. And you can't sue me because you'll be unemployed if I'm shut down."

"This is true." She kicks my leg with her foot. "Relax. I won't sue you for raccoon boob assault. But I need a couple of new scrub tops. He's torn the neckline on every single one I own."

"Order them and use the sanctuary credit card."

"Maybe I'll order my new t-shirt, too. Tate has a graphic designer friend who's making me a 'Ricky was here' design."

"I forbid you to wear that on sanctuary grounds."

"You're no fun."

Ricky's eyes drift closed. His body rises and falls with Maren's breathing. One paw rests on her collarbone, the other tucked under him. For a moment, everything is still. Her breathing deepens, and he's a warm loaf of furry contentment.

Then I see it. His left paw, the one on her collarbone, is moving, creeping south an inch at a time, his fingers spreading wide as they slide down from bone to the soft curve below it. His paw opens, flexes, and gives one deliberate squeeze.

Maren's eyes fly open. She looks down at him, then over at me.

"Did he just honk my boob?"

I press my lips together so hard my teeth ache.

Ricky's eyes are still closed. His face is the picture of pure, undisturbed, innocent slumber. His paw squeezes again.

"Oh, for Christ's sake." Maren pulls his hand away and tucks it against his side. "Give it a rest, perv."

I snort and tilt my head back on the cushion, closing my eyes and sighing.

Maren was right.

We created a boob monster.

Damien - Bonus Scene

I crest the hill, and the valley opens up below me. I haven't been back to Aspen Ridge since the night I killed Nash. The blood is gone, bleach and time erasing it from the stainless steel as if it had never happened. Cade disposed of Nash's body per our protocols, never to be seen again. The elk he butchered got better burials.

As I drive down Main Street, the post office sign reminds me I haven't stopped in since the day I closed on the Morrison estate. Like most properties up here in the middle of nowhere, it doesn't have a mailbox. The postal service doesn't deliver to the property. It's too remote, too far off the main road, and now too tangled in the county's bureaucratic hesitation to grant me a proper address designation.

I pull over in front of Nancy's Diner and sit for a moment with my hands on the wheel.

The face in the rearview mirror belongs to a man who bought a serial killer's house. A man with two faces. One human and one wolf. A businessman whose suit is gone today, replaced by a button-down shirt and black pants, but the performance is the same. I push my hair back from my forehead, check that the silver at my temples reads distinguished rather than disheveled, and head across the street.

The bell above the post office door announces me with a bright, tinny chime.

The interior is small and cool, smelling of old paper and the industrial cleaner they use on the linoleum. There's one service window at the back, a wall of brass boxes to the left, and a community bulletin board to the right, pinned thick with flyers for firewood delivery and lost cats and a pancake breakfast at the church.

Eleanor is behind the counter. I've met her once before, the day I came in to set up the box, though I never get any mail here. She'd talked for twenty minutes straight while I filled out a single form.

She's sorting a stack of catalogs, her rhinestone-studded glasses perched on her nose, her jet-black hair piled in a loose bun that defies both gravity and her age. She has to be pushing eighty. I'd bet my fortune that hair hasn't been its natural color since Reagan's first term.

She lifts her head before I've taken three steps, as if the bell told her everything she needed to know about who walked in.

"If it isn't the mystery man from the Morrison place."

"Good morning, Eleanor. Please call me Damien."

"Oh." She presses a hand to her chest, rhinestones catching the fluorescent light and scattering tiny prisms across the wall of boxes. "Frank, did you hear that? He remembers my name."

A grunt comes from the back room. Frank appears in the doorway behind the counter, a hefty balding man who has to be at least several inches shorter than his wife.

"Ahh, Mr. Wolfe, nice to see you again."

"Frank." I nod my head at him. "Please call me Damien."

He grabs a bin of packages from under the counter and retreats to the back again without another word.

Eleanor watches him go with a fond exasperation. "Don't mind Frank. He's been grumpy since 1987. I think it was a Wednesday." She leans across the counter, the catalogs forgotten. "So. How's the renovation coming? I heard the county's giving you fits with the permits."

"News travels fast."

"Honey, news doesn't travel in Aspen Ridge. It's already everywhere." She pushes her glasses up with one finger. "With that house's history. People are curious. You can't blame them."

I keep my expression pleasant. The performance requires so little effort it barely registers as effort at all.

"The house is a project. Projects take time."

"A project?" Eleanor's eyebrow arches. "That's one word for it. Frank drove a couple of packages up to Luna's place last week and said the house still looks like it wants to eat people."

"You can't see the house from the road."

"Oh, he drove down the driveway. Frank's curiosity gets the better of him sometimes." She looks over her shoulder. "Doesn't it, honey?"

Another grunt echoes from the back room.

"See? He agrees with me." Eleanor turns back to me. "Now. Your box is 214. Nothing in it, I'm afraid. You're either the most boring man in Colorado or the most secretive." She studies me over her glasses. "I'm betting on the second one."

"You'd lose that bet. I'm a very boring man."

"Now, I don't believe that for a minute." She gives me a long look that says she's been alive long enough to know better. "So are you up there all alone in that big old horror movie house? No wife? Girlfriend? Boyfriend? I don't judge."

"Just me and my dog."

"A dog person. Good. That's a point in your favor." She taps the counter with one coral-painted fingernail. "Animal people fit in real well up here."

I reach into my pocket, pull out a card, and set it on the counter between us. "If anything does come in for me, I'd appreciate a call."

She tucks it into her blouse pocket without looking at it. "Be happy to."

"Eleanor, Frank." I call toward the back as I head for the door. "Always a pleasure."

"The pleasure is all mine, honey. Frank doesn't feel pleasure anymore. It's part of his condition."

A muffled "I can hear you" drifts from the back room.

I push the door open with one hand. The resistance on the other side registers a half-second too late.

The door swings outward and connects with a body. A small body. The impact is solid enough that I see a flash of blonde hair and eyes going wide before she stumbles backward. My hand shoots out on reflex, but she's already catching herself on the harness she has in her hand.

She's one foot away.

Close enough that I catch the scent of peaches and antiseptic and the warm, clean scent of sun on bare skin. The knot at the back of her head is coming loose, wisps of blonde hair framing a face free of makeup and hazel eyes, green and gold in the late afternoon light. Her mouth is half-open with an apology.

"I'm sor—"

A low growl rumbles from the wolf attached to that harness, and she looks down at him, hand dropping to his head.

"Easy, boy."

My lungs refuse to expand.

The world narrows to her. The wolf. The way her body curves around the animal, protective and tender. The same posture I watched through rain and lightning over a month ago when she carried a wounded creature against her chest.

My body makes the decision before my brain does, putting distance between us before the part of me that has other ideas gets a vote. My shoes hit the pavement in long, measured strides, carrying me straight across the street, past the Range Rover and through the door of Nancy's Diner because walking away is the only safe option.

The place is half-full, the hiss and sizzle of a griddle grating against my eardrums. A waitress with a coffee pot and a tired smile looks up.

"Cheeseburger. Medium-rare. To go."

She blinks. "You want to sit, or—"

"I'll wait over here."

She shrugs and disappears into the kitchen. I take a position at the front window, hands in my pockets, jaw set, eyes fixed on the post office door across the street.

I count the minutes. Ten of them pass before the post office door opens again, and she steps out, her wolf at her hip, those loose strands of blonde hair catching the breeze. She fishes for her truck keys with one hand, her lips moving in a quiet conversation with the wolf. Then she looks around like she can feel someone watching her.

My hands curl into fists inside my pockets.

This is not the plan. The plan is the Morrison estate. The plan is the kill room and the mask and the ledger of names that Cade feeds me one by one. The plan is isolation. A fortress on a ridge, surrounded by five hundred acres of silence, where the wolf can work without interference. I bought this property because it sits at the edge of the world, because no one goes there, because the nearest neighbor is...

Her.

My reflection stares back at me from the window, superimposed on the almost empty road. A face built for boardrooms and charity galas and the careful maintenance of a lie.

Behind that face, the wolf paces, restless.

"Order's ready." The waitress sets a paper bag on the counter behind me.

I drop a hundred without turning around and grab it.

Outside, my neighbor climbs into her truck, settles the wolf in the passenger seat, and pulls out of her parking spot with the careful attention of a woman who has driven mountain roads her whole life. I step out of the diner as she looks in the rearview mirror, her gaze holding on me for a beat before she drives away.

Then she's gone, and the street is just a street again, ordinary and flat.

I came to Aspen Ridge for the clean simplicity of predator and prey and the dark meting out of justice. Not for a woman with golden hair falling out of a messy knot and a wolf companion. Not for hazel eyes that shift from green to gold. And not for the tightening behind my ribs that returns now, stronger than before, an unexplainable gravitational pull drawing me in.

The smart move is to stay in my lane, keep to my plan, and adhere to the rules I set in place twenty-five years ago. Let Cade bring me the next name. Keep the walls high and the distance absolute.

But perhaps some things are worth breaking the rules for.

Thank You

Thank you for spending time in this world. I know you came for the raccoon, and I hope he delivered. Ricky is the kind of creature who leaves a mark on everyone he meets, usually in the form of scratches in the boob region and a story they'll tell for years, and I hope a little of that transfers onto the page.

Wildlife rehabilitation is hard, underfunded, and largely invisible work. The people who do it open their homes, their hearts, and occasionally their shirts to animals that need them. They cancel plans, lose sleep, and hand-feed a baby animal every two hours without once asking for credit, because the alternative is unthinkable. They deserve more than they get. If this book sends you looking for a sanctuary to support, Ricky has done his job. He always was an overachiever, face-first into everything he loved.

And if it just makes you laugh until you cry, well. He'll take that too.

Please Review

Reviews are kind of a big deal for indie authors.

They help books get discovered, build momentum, and find their way to readers who might actually love them. They're one of the most powerful ways you can support an author, and trust me, we notice and appreciate every single one.

So if you enjoyed WATCH OVER ME (A WATCHED IN DARKNESS PREQUEL NOVELLA), I'd be incredibly grateful if you'd leave a review on Amazon, Goodreads, and/or wherever you share your reading recommendations. Even a few sentences go a long way.

Thank you so much for your support—it truly means the world!

Below are easy links for you.

Amazon

Goodreads

BookBub

Follow Me

For previews, deleted scenes and goodies, sign up for my newsletter:
Sign Up Here
https://vehuntley.com/

Connect with V.E:
https://www.facebook.com/v.e.huntley.author
https://www.instagram.com/vehuntley/
https://x.com/vehuntleywriter
https://www.tiktok.com/@vehuntley
https://bsky.app/profile/vehuntleyauthor.bsky.social
https://www.pinterest.com/vehuntleywriter/
https://www.goodreads.com/author/show/50245965.V_E_Huntley
Join my Whispers After Dark Facebook Group—it's a place we can talk about all things books, especially naughty things
https://www.facebook.com/groups/v.e.huntleys.whispers.after.dark

Books by V.E. Huntley

The BloodStone Legacy Series

Damnation

Atonement

Redemption

Watched in Darkness Series

Watch Me Break

Watch Me Burn

Watch Over Me Prequel Novella

Watch Me Bleed—Coming 2027

Sacred Sins—Coming 2027

Shadow Ice Brotherhood Series

Frozen Fury—Coming 2027

Frozen Wrath—Coming 2028

Frozen Savage—TBD

Frozen Sins—TBD

Frozen Vengeance—TBD

Frozen Menace—TBD

Strike & Surrender Series

Strike Hard, Surrender Softly—Coming 2027

Strike High, Surrender Deep—Coming 2028

Strike First, Surrender Last—TBD

Strike Fast, Surrender Slow—TBD

Strike Once, Surrender Forever—TBD

Strike Strong, Surrender Sweet—TBD

Acknowledgements

There are never enough words for this page, which is ironic given my profession, but here we go.

Chris, my hubby, my person, the man who has learned to feed himself more often than not and has never once complained about it to my face. Your love and support are the reason any of this exists. Thank you.

Elle, my editor, who will tell me the truth even when I don't want to hear it, and whose notes have made every single book better than it would have been without her. Thank you for your honesty.

To my readers, who found these twisted little stories and decided to stay. You're the reason I keep going. I have so many more stories to tell you, and I cannot wait.

And to my parents, up in whatever corner of heaven has the best view of my laptop screen. You built me, which means this is technically your fault. You read to me, encouraged me, and told me I could do anything, and I want you to know I took that very literally. Nan, I'm aware the spicy parts of my books would make you put them down and say the rosary. Gramps, I suspect you would have read a few pages, then handed it back without making eye contact. I miss you both every day. And I can hear you up there, clear as anything, turning to each other and saying, "This is your fault."

About the author

I 'm a retired producer who's spent most of my life telling stories in one form or another. Just ask my cats—they've endured years of me reciting entire dialogue scenes to them when all they desperately wanted was a nap.

My childhood fear of Dracula was so intense I couldn't sleep without the lights on and my mother standing guard at my bedroom door. Fast forward a few decades, and that terror has morphed into a full-blown obsession with all things dark and twisted.

After more than twenty years in film and television, I decided to follow my true calling—writing dark, steamy romance about anti-heroes who swear too much and have serious anger management issues, and the strong, spirited heroines who refuse to put up with their nonsense (but love them anyway).

When I'm not writing, I'm watching movies, reading, traveling, or adding to my husband's never-ending honey-do list (it's basically a part-time job at this point). You can find out more about me on my website, www.vehuntley.com.